✳ LINKING ENGLISH ✳

讀李家同學英文 7

李家同◎著

Nick Hawkins（郝凱揚）◎譯、解析

A Little Boy's Dad
小男孩的爸爸

透過李家同簡潔而寓意深遠的文章，領略用英文表達中文故事的妙趣

小男孩的爸爸◎考試◎大作家的夢想◎苦工◎鐘聲又再響起

那青草覆地的墓園◎小銀盒子

序

李家同

我真該謝謝郝凱揚先生將我的文章譯成了英文。這當然不是一件簡單的事情，但是我看了他的翻譯，我發現他的翻譯絕對是正確的，而且非常優美。外國人寫的小說，往往用字非常艱難。對一般人而言，都太難了。這本書比較容易，沒有用太難的字。郝先生是美國人，能做這件事情，充分展現他的中英文造詣很高，他一定是一位非常聰明的人。

這一本書最大的好處是有對英文的註解、也有練習，想學英文的年輕人可以從註解中學到很多英文的基本學問。

我在此給讀者一個建議：你不妨先看看中文文章，先不看英文的翻譯，然後試著將中文翻成英文，我相信你一定會覺得中翻英好困難。譯完以後，再去看郝先生的翻譯，相信你可以學到不少，也可以寫出越來越像外國人寫的句子。

我尤其希望讀者注意標點符號的用法。英文的標點符號是非常重要的，中文句子對標點符號的標準比較寬鬆，但英文絕對不行，一個標點符號用錯了，全句的結構就是錯了。讀者可以利用這個機會好好地學會如何正確地下英文的標點符號。

另外，千萬要注意動詞的用法，如果你英文動詞沒有用錯，你的英文就很厲害了。信不信由你，英文不好的人常常不會用現在完成式，可是這本書裡用了很多的現在完成式，你不妨仔細研究為什麼要用這種我們中國人所不熟悉的時態。

在英文句子裡，一定要有一個主詞和一個動詞，讀者不妨在每一個句子裡去找一下，主詞和動詞一定會存在。我們中國人有時寫一個英文句子，但是句子中，主詞和動詞弄不清楚，以至於有的動詞沒有主詞。也就因為如此，凡是這種主詞和動詞關係不清楚的句子，意思也會弄不清楚。讀者如果覺得這些文章很容易懂，其實完全是因為每一個句子的主詞和動詞都很清楚的原因。

如果你有時不知道如何用英文表達你的想法，你應該知道，這是正常的事。多看這本書，對你一定有幫助。

看這本書的時候，再次建議你先看中文，立刻試譯，再參考英譯。這樣做，對你的英文作文會有很大的好處。

最後我謝謝郝凱揚，他的註解使這本書生色不少。當然我也該謝謝聯經出版公司，我相信這本書的出版會有助於很多想學好英文的年輕人，這本書能夠順利出現，林載爵先生和何采嬪女士有很大的功勞，我在此謝謝他們。

起而行

郝凱揚

李家同令人敬佩的地方，不在於他淵博的學問，也不在於他虔誠的信仰。我之所以佩服他，是因為他將他的理想付諸行動。

眾人皆知，李教授信奉的是天主教，而且他以他的信仰為寫作的出發點。在台灣，即使把天主教、基督教和摩門教三大派基督徒的人數全部加起來，所佔的比例還不到人口的一成。那麼，一個天主教徒寫的書怎麼會在台灣的社會廣受歡迎呢？關鍵在於「付諸行動」四個字。

幾年前，我在台灣當過兩年的傳教士。當我問人家「你有什麼宗教信仰」時，最常聽到的一句話是「所有的宗教都是勸人為善」。其實我並非不知道，說這句話的用意是以較為委婉的口氣拒絕我，但這十一個字所蘊含的意義非常深遠。儒家的「仁義」、道家的「道」、佛教的「慈悲」、基督徒的「博愛」、甚至無神論的「倫理」，宗旨都不外乎教人把內在的善性發揮出來。然而光說好聽的話沒有用——真正的信徒一定要實踐他的信仰，否則他只是個偽善者。李家同主要不是個作者，乃是個「做者」：文作得少，事做得多。也就是因為如此，才有這麼多的讀者閱讀他的書，並從中得到感動。

　　「實踐」是個極為管用的通則，我們不妨想想它如何適用在語言的學習上。假如一個人（我們不說他是誰）訂了一年的美語雜誌，每個月固定讀一本上好的英文教材，但他從來不寫半個英文字，也不說半句英語，試問，他的英文能力會突飛猛進嗎？他對自己的英文能力會有很大的信心嗎？我再來做另一個假設：倘若另一個人（我們依然不說他是誰）買不起最好的英文教材，但他喜歡跟幾個不會中文的外國朋友見面，也喜歡寫英文日記或部落格，那麼英文會不會豐富他的人生？他會不會比較容易記住他所學的東西？

　　你自己比較像這兩個人中的哪一個？如果你的答案令你不滿，你要如何改變你學英文的方式？以我學中文的經驗來說，我覺得最重要的是給自己一個愛學的理由和非練習不可的環境。愛學的理由可以好玩（想唱美國的流行音樂）；文雅（更能欣賞英國文學）；不良（可以搭訕外國女生）；實際（要跟國外的客戶做生意）；無聊（愛挑布希總統的語病）等等，找出自己的理由應該不難。尋找非練習不可的環境對無法長期出國的人可能沒那麼容易，可是並非不可能——除了以上提過的，和不會中文的外國人交朋友以及利用網路寫英文部落格，還有別的方法。還有，在學會講英文的過程中，一定要多出一些難堪的錯，發現了之後笑一笑自己，因為這樣才算豁了出去。如果你因為怕出糗而只講最簡單的英文，怎麼會進步？你又不是沒聽過四聲不準的外國學生說「我恨矮台灣人」（我很愛台灣人）啦！

　　最後我想說，我絕對不是個隨隨便便的譯者和解析者——把這些精采的故事譯成傳神的英文花了我不少心思。目的只有一個——希望你能藉此體會到學英文的樂趣！至於進步，我只能提供好的資源——要不要好好利用，完全由你決定了。

目次
CONTENTS

A Little Boy's Dad
小男孩的爸爸

1-5　　林教授是我們電機系的教授，他是一個典型的電機系教授，從小就一切順利，別人考高中送掉半條命，林教授在全無補習之下，輕鬆地考進了明星高中，然後就一帆風順，碩士後三年，就拿到了博士學位，說實話，他的指導教授雖然是一位大牌教授，但根本弄不清楚他的博士論文是怎麼一回事。

　　可是林教授卻有一件事不太順利，他雖然有了未婚妻，卻好久沒有結婚，似乎他的未婚妻老是拖三拉四的，不論他如何努力，他的未婚妻始終不給他確定的結婚時間。

　　有一天，我在研究室裡，忽然接到了林教授的電話，他說他在埔里的麥當勞遭遇到了大麻煩，叫我趕快去救他一命。我趕到了麥當勞，發現他在照顧一個小男孩吃霜淇淋。這個小孩黑黑的，大眼睛，可愛極了。林教授看到我以後，安撫了一下小男孩，叫他繼續一個人吃，然後走過來，輕輕地告訴我一個好滑稽的故事。

CD1-2
- ◇ faculty (n.) 教職員（全體）
- ◇ typical (adj.) 典型的；具代表性的
- ◇ EE (n.) Electrical Engineering 電機學系的縮寫
- ◇ ultra- (字頭.) 極端；非常
- ◇ smooth (adj.) 順利的
- ◇ sail (v.) 航行
- ◇ earn (n.) 掙得
- ◇ MS（Master of Science）(n.) 碩士學位
- ◇ hotshot (n.) 厲害角色
- ◇ wrap (v.) 包起來
- ◇ dissertation (n.)（高等學位的）論文
- ◇ fiancée (n.) 未婚妻（注意：未婚夫＝fiancé，發音相同，卻少了最後的 e）

1-5
CD1-1

Professor Lin is on the faculty of our electrical engineering department. He's a typical EE professor in that success has always come easily for him: while others worked themselves half to death studying for high school entrance exams, Professor Lin got into an ultra-elite high school without even a minute of cram school. From then on it was smooth sailing: he earned his Ph.D. just three years after his MS. Honestly, even the hotshot professor he had for an adviser couldn't wrap his head around his dissertation.

But there was one thing in Professor Lin's life that wasn't going so smoothly: he and his longtime fiancée had never tied the knot. His fiancée, it seemed, was dragging her feet: no matter how hard he tried, she refused to set a date for their wedding.

One day while I was in the lab, I got an unexpected call from Professor Lin. He said he had run into big trouble at the McDonald's in Puli and required my immediate assistance. I rushed over to McDonald's, where I found him accompanied by a little boy eating an ice cream cone. With his dark skin and big eyes, the boy looked adorable. When he saw me, Professor Lin told the boy to relax and keep eating by himself. Then he walked over to me and, lowering his voice, recounted his amusing story.

◈ tie (v.) 打（結）
◈ knot (n.) 結
◈ drag (v.) 拖
◈ run into (v.) 碰到；遇到
◈ assistance (n.) 協助
◈ rush (v.) 趕

◈ over (adv.) 從一邊到另一邊
◈ accompany (v.) 陪伴
◈ relax (v.) 放鬆
◈ recount (v.) 敘述
◈ amusing (adj.) 詼諧的；有趣的

　　林教授說他今天來麥當勞吃漢堡，在排隊的時候，忽然有一個小鬼拉他的褲子，叫他「爸爸」。他被這個小鬼叫了爸爸，只好請他不要再叫了，沒有想到這個小鬼一點都不為所動，反而越叫越大聲，令林教授窘不堪言。有一位胖女人，一聽到林教授否認他是小鬼的爸爸，氣得不得了，她帶了一把傘，就拿起傘來打林教授的頭。林教授發現情勢不妙，趕緊替小鬼點吃的東西，陪他吃飯。現在飯已經吃完了，他又點了霜淇淋給他吃。

　　林教授問我該怎麼辦？我首先問他究竟是不是這個小男孩的爸爸，林教授一再地否認，他說他也不是任何小孩的爸爸。他還說，實在迫不得已，他可以利用 DNA 檢驗來證明他完全是被小男孩栽贓的。

6-10　　我說我們唯一該做的事情就是將小男孩送到派出所，林教授同意了。他將小孩抱起來，因為這個小孩已經睡著了。到了警察局，林教授一字不提這個小孩叫他爸爸的事，只說他發現這個孩子走丟了。員警說已經有人報了案，這個孩子的媽媽病重，爸爸已經去世，孩子由阿姨看著的，但是媽媽在埔里基督教醫院的加護病房，阿姨一不小

◇ rascal (n.) 流氓；調皮的小孩
◇ grab hold of (v.) 抓住
◇ chagrin (n.) 窘態
◇ whereupon (adv.) 於是
◇ deny (v.) 否認
◇ swing (v.) 轉動（注意不規則的過去式）

According to Professor Lin, he had come to McDonald's for a hamburger, but as he was waiting in line, suddenly a little rascal grabbed hold of his pant leg and called him "Daddy." Under the circumstances, all he could do was ask the boy not to call him Daddy anymore. But the boy was unmoved by this request—in fact, it only made him shout louder, much to Professor Lin's chagrin. Whereupon a fat woman, hearing Professor Lin deny that he was the boy's father, lost her temper and swung the umbrella she was carrying at his head. Realizing that he was trapped, Professor Lin hurriedly ordered some food for the boy and sat down to eat with him. Once they finished eating, he ordered him an ice cream cone.

"What should I do?" Professor Lin asked. First off, I asked him if he really was the boy's dad. Professor Lin vigorously denied having ever fathered any children. He even said that if worst came to worst, he could do a DNA test to prove he had been "falsely accused" by the boy.

I said that all we could do was take the boy over to the local police station. Professor Lin agreed. He picked up the little boy, now fast asleep, and carried him there. At the station, Professor Lin never mentioned anything about the boy calling him Daddy—he just said he had discovered that he was lost. The boy had already been reported missing, the officer said: his mother was seriously ill and his father was dead. He was looked after by his aunt, but his mother was in

6-10

◇ trapped (adj.) 被困住的
◇ hurriedly (adv.) 匆匆
◇ vigorously (adv.) 強有力地
◇ accuse (v.) 控訴
◇ fast asleep (adj.) 熟睡的
◇ missing (adj.) 失蹤了

心，孩子就溜到街上了。現在總算被我們找到了，員警也很高興。

員警認得我，叫我簽了字，答應儘速將小孩送回埔里去，我們到了埔里基督教醫院。孩子的阿姨看到孩子回來了，鬆了一口氣。她一再感謝林教授，也告訴我們孩子的媽媽已經昏迷，去世大概僅僅是時間的問題了。孩子呢？他不太懂這是怎麼一回事，他只是緊緊地抱住林教授不放，林教授打了個電話給他的研究生，說他有事，無法和他們見面，然後又給了我一個工作，要我到公車站去將他的未婚妻接到醫院來。

林教授的未婚妻聽了這個故事，覺得好好玩，她認為這事簡直有點不可思議，怎麼會有小孩子無緣無故地叫陌生人爸爸？我說也許他們有緣，這一點林教授的未婚妻很快地就發現了，她親眼看到孩子和林教授難分難捨的景象。

不久以後，林教授和他的未婚妻參加了孩子媽媽的葬禮，林教授第一次聽到原住民的聖歌，大為感動，反正他已是他們家庭的一份子，孩子已經不能離開他了，也離不開林教授的未婚妻。

◇ intensive care unit (n.) 加護病房，簡稱 ICU
◇ wander (v.) 亂跑
◇ breathe (v.) 呼氣
◇ sigh (n.) 嘆氣
◇ relief (n.) 如釋重負的安慰
◇ warmly (adv.) 熱情地
◇ coma (n.) 昏迷的狀態
◇ practically (adv.) 簡直
◇ destiny (n.) 命運

the intensive care unit at Puli Christian Hospital, and in a moment of inattention, the aunt had let him wander out on the street. The policeman was very pleased to see that we had found him again.

The officer, who knew me, asked me to sign a form and promise to return the boy to Puli Christian Hospital as soon as possible. We arrived at the hospital; seeing her nephew return, the boy's aunt breathed a sigh of relief. Even as she warmly thanked Professor Lin, she told us that the boy's mother was in a coma and her death was only a matter of time. As for the little boy, he didn't understand what a coma was—he just held tightly to Professor Lin. The professor called his graduate students to let them know he wouldn't be able to meet with them as planned.

Professor Lin's fiancée was highly amused by the story. In her opinion, it was practically unbelievable—since when do little boys call strangers Daddy for no reason? Perhaps their destinies were somehow intertwined, I suggested. She soon discovered that that was indeed the case: she saw with her own eyes how attached the boy and Professor Lin had become.

Not long after, Professor Lin and his fiancée attended the boy's mother's funeral. It was the first time Professor Lin had heard hymns sung by aborigines, and he was greatly moved. At any rate, the boy was part of their family now: he couldn't bear to part with Professor Lin or his fiancée.

◈ intertwined (adj.) 交纏在一起的
◈ attached (adj.) 依戀的
◈ aborigines (n.) 原住民

◈ bear (v.) 忍受
◈ part (v.) 分離

　　林教授說他已經決定正式收養這小孩子，小孩子現在的監護人是他的阿姨，她毫無意見地答應了。南投縣社會局派人到暨大調查林教授的為人，我們這些同事當然是異口同聲地將林教授講得不能再好。果真林教授得到了一份南投縣社會局的公文，他們原則上同意林教授正式收養那個男孩子，唯一的條件是他必須在三個月內結婚，如果他在三個月內仍是單身漢，他們就要考慮別人了。

11-15　　我們都替林教授捏了一把冷汗，試想他的未婚妻一直不肯確定結婚的日期，這次又如何會答應呢？沒有想到林教授的未婚妻立刻就答應了。

　　婚禮在小孩子山地家鄉的教堂裡進行，我們都去觀禮，新郎在祭壇前等新娘，第一個進來的卻是那個小男孩，他穿了一套全新的深色西裝，打了一個紅色的領結，一面走，一面撒花，我們大家不約而同地站了起來，大家都要看這個可愛的小男孩的風采。新娘走進來的時候，我們才將注意力轉移到新娘那裡去。

◇ adopt (v.) 收養
◇ hesitation (n.) 猶豫
◇ guardian (n.) 監護人
◇ investigate (v.) 調查
◇ colleague (n.) 同僚
◇ praise (n.) 讚美

◇ official (adj.) 官方的
◇ notify (v.) 通知
◇ condition (n.) 條件
◇ sweat (v.) 流 (汗)
◇ bullet (n.) 子彈
◇ chapel (n.) 教堂

Professor Lin announced that he had decided to formally adopt the boy. Without hesitation, the boy's current guardian—his aunt—agreed. The Nantou County Department of Social Affairs sent someone to National Chi Nan University to investigate Professor Lin's character; it goes without saying that his colleagues, myself included, had nothing but praise for him. As expected, Professor Lin received an official letter from the DSA notifying him that he had been approved to formally adopt the boy—on condition that he married within the next three months. If he was still single after three months, they would have to consider someone else.

We all sweat bullets on Professor Lin's behalf. After all, his fiancée   11-15 had always refused to set a date in the past—why would she do so now? To our surprise, however, she said yes without hesitation.

The wedding was held at a chapel in the boy's hometown in the mountains; all of us were there. As the groom awaited the bride in front of the altar, the first person to walk in was the little boy. Dressed in a brand-new dark suit with a red bow tie, he scattered flowers as he walked. With one accord, the audience rose to its feet, hoping to catch a glimpse of the cute little boy in his moment of glory. Only when the bride walked in did we shift our attention to her.

⬥ await (v.) 等待（稍嫌正式，注意之後不用加 for）
⬥ altar (n.) 祭壇
⬥ brand-new (adj.) 嶄新的
⬥ scatter (v.) 撒

⬥ with one accord (adv.) 全體一致；不約而同
⬥ catch a glimpse of (v.) 瞥見
⬥ glory (n.) 光榮
⬥ shift (v.) 轉移

我們都替林氏夫婦高興，因為他們平白地有了一個四歲的兒子，一年以後，他們的小孩也誕生了，是個白白胖胖的小女娃。

現在，林教授的小女兒也會走路了，我們常常看到林教授夫婦在黃昏時帶著他們的兩個頑皮小孩在暨大的草地上玩，他們還養了一隻狗，看孩子們在草地上跑來跑去，有時在追蝴蝶，有時在追校園裡到處都有的白鷺鷥，任何人都會打從心靈深處感到溫暖。春天來了，校園裡一百株的羊蹄甲花盛開，林教授的女兒常常在樹下撿從樹上掉下來的粉紅色花瓣，沒有比這個景象再美的了。

我呢？總覺得這個故事發展得太過完滿，世界上不可能有這樣完滿的故事的。有一天，我閒來無事，將整個故事從頭到尾想了一遍，然後我發了一封電子郵件給林教授。

16-20　　不久，電話鈴就響了，林教授說他要到我研究室來看我，我知道為什麼他要來，他是來招認了。

我準備了一壺咖啡，林教授喝了一杯咖啡以後，坦白地承認孩子當

◇ charge (n.) 費用
◇ give birth to (v.) 生出
◇ rambunctious (adj.) 調皮的
◇ along with (prep.) 還有
◇ chase (v.) 追
◇ ubiquitous (adj.) 到處都有的
◇ thoroughly (adv.) 徹底
◇ in full bloom (adj.) (花) 盛開

We were all happy for the Lins, who now had a four-year-old son, free of charge. A year later, they gave birth to a child of their own, a plump, white baby girl.

Now that Professor Lin's little daughter has learned to walk, in the evening we often see the Lins playing with their two rambunctious children on the grass of Chi Nan University, along with their pet dog. Watching the kids run around on the grass chasing butterflies or the white egrets so ubiquitous on campus is enough to thoroughly warm anyone's heart. Spring has come; the hundred orchid trees on campus are in full bloom, and Professor Lin's daughter likes to gather up the pink petals that fall from the trees. There couldn't be a more beautiful scene.

As for myself, I always felt like that the way everything had turned out was too perfect—such a perfect story couldn't possibly happen in this world. So one day, when I had a little free time, I thought carefully through the story from beginning to end, and then I sent an email to Professor Lin.

A short time later, the telephone rang: Professor Lin said he was on his way to the lab to see me. I knew the purpose of his visit: he was coming to confess. 16-20

After he'd had a cup of the coffee I'd prepared, Professor Lin admitted frankly that the boy had not called him Daddy that day.

◈ petal (n.) 花瓣
◈ turn out (v.) 結果是
◈ confess (v.) 供認
◈ admit (v.) 承認
◈ frankly (adv.) 坦白地

初沒有叫他爸爸，孩子走失了，在哭。林教授問他爸爸在哪裡，孩子說：「爸爸走了。」然後又告訴林教授他的媽媽在加護病房。我們的林教授靈機一動，一面買東西給小孩吃，一面編了一個感人的故事來騙我這個糊塗老頭。他沒有想到我會寄一封電子郵件給他，而這封電子郵件只有一句話：「林大教授，孩子究竟有沒有叫你爸爸？」他一看就知道我已經識穿了他的把戲。

雖然林教授承認他亂編故事，但他仍嘴硬，他說他一眼就愛上了這個大眼睛的小男孩，現在如願以償地結了婚，也做成了孩子的爸爸，可見他的規劃多偉大。他只有一個疑問，我如何知道他亂編故事的？

我告訴他，他的故事自始至終沒有人證，他和我講孩子叫他爸爸的時候，聲音極小，旁邊的人都聽不見，那個小男孩正全神貫注地吃霜淇淋，所以也聽不見他未來的爸爸在說什麼。最嚴重的是：他說有一位胖女人用傘打他，那天是冬天，天氣非常好，沒有雨，太陽也不辣，沒有人會帶傘的，這是他故事的一大漏洞。

◈ poignant (adj.) 很感人的
◈ deceive (v.) 矇騙 (名詞形式為 deception)
◈ gullible (adj.) 好騙
◈ yours truly (n.) (俚) 我
◈ consist of (v.) 由……構成
◈ unrepentant (adj.) 沒有悔意的

◈ brilliance (n.) 聰明才智
◈ figure out (v.) 弄清楚；識破
◈ back up (v.) 支持
◈ whisper (n.) 耳語
◈ exclusively (adj.) 專門地、全神貫注地

He was just lost, and crying. When Professor Lin asked him where his daddy was, the boy replied, "He passed away." Then he told Professor Lin that his mom was in the ICU. Suddenly Professor Lin had an idea: as he bought some food for the boy, he made up a poignant story to deceive the gullible old man that is yours truly. He never thought I would send him an email about it. The email I sent consisted of a single sentence: "So, great Professor Lin, did the boy really call you 'Daddy' that day?" As soon as he saw it, he knew I had seen through his deception.

Although Professor Lin admitted having made the story up, he was unrepentant. It only took one look for him to fall in love with the wide-eyed little boy, he said. Not only had he succeeded in marrying the woman he loved, but he had become a little boy's dad as well, which proved the brilliance of his plan. His only question was, how had I figured out the truth?

I told him it was because he had no witnesses to back up any part of his story. When he got to the part about the boy calling him "Daddy," he had lowered his voice to almost a whisper, so that none of the people around us could hear what he was saying. Even the little boy didn't hear what his future dad was saying, his attention being focused exclusively on the ice cream cone in his hand. But the real giveaway was the part about the fat lady swinging her umbrella at him. It was winter that day, and the weather had been beautiful: no rain, just gentle sunlight. No one would have carried an umbrella on a day like that—it was a big flaw in his story.

◈ giveaway (n.) 洩漏真相的東西　　　◈ flaw (n.) 瑕疵

林教授表示他不在意我拆穿了他美麗而充滿愛心的謊言，卻不知不覺地又倒了一杯咖啡喝，其實他多多少少有些緊張的。

21-22　至於林太太呢？她說她早就知道林教授在亂編故事，她之所以好久沒有和林教授結婚，也就是因為林教授特別會亂編故事，有的時候，她簡直弄不清楚林教授講的是故事，還是事實。那個事件以後，她發現林教授心腸非常好，只是有時有點狡猾，可是狡猾都是為了開玩笑，沒有任何惡意，她的想法是一個如此有慈悲心的人，將來一定會是個好丈夫，於是就結婚了。果真，林教授不僅僅是個好丈夫，也是個好爸爸。

所以，我錯了。世界上的確可能有完美事情的。林教授自以為他聰明過人，只要能編出一個將未婚妻騙得團團轉的故事，一切就很美滿。其實不然，他的故事發展得如此之好，是因為他是個好人，好人常會有美滿家庭的，以後我要常常將林教授的故事告訴我的學生。告訴他們一定要先做一個好人，然後自然會有一個美滿家庭。

◇ unwittingly（adv.）不知不覺地
◇ pour（v.）倒（液體）
◇ betray（v.）透露；顯示出（注意，這裡並沒有「背叛」的意思）
◇ all along（adv.）一直以來
◇ fib（n.）沒有傷害的小謊
◇ tall tale（n.）誇張不實的故事
◇ episode（n.）事件

Even as he claimed he didn't care that I had seen through his beautiful, charitable lie, he unwittingly poured himself another cup of coffee, thus betraying a certain amount of nervousness.

As for Mrs. Lin, she said she had known all along that Professor 21-22 Lin had made the story up. That was the reason why she had waited so long to marry the professor; he loved to tell fibs, to the point that sometimes she had a hard time discerning whether he was telling the truth or just another tall tale. After the episode with the boy, however, she realized that Professor Lin had a very good heart—he just liked to stretch the truth a bit. But he only stretched the truth to joke around, never to do harm. She figured that such a compassionate man would surely make a good husband, so she married him. And she was right—Professor Lin turned out to be not just a good husband, but a good father too.

So, I was wrong—perfect stories do happen in this world. Being rather cleverer than most men, Professor Lin thought that if he made up a story that thoroughly tricked his fiancée, everything would turn out wonderfully. In fact, the real reason everything had turned out so well was that he was a good man, and good men almost always have happy families. After that, I often told Professor Lin's story to my students to convince them that if they wanted to have happy families, they should be good people first.

◈ stretch (v.) 扭曲
◈ joke around (v.) 開玩笑
◈ compassionate (adj.) 慈悲的

◈ clever (adj.) 精明
◈ trick (v.) 騙
◈ convince (v.) 說服

（1）faculty（全體教職員）的用法（1段）

Professor Lin is on the faculty of our electrical engineering department.
林教授是我們電機系的教授。

解析

如同前面單字註腳所示，faculty 指的是在特定的學系或大學中自成一群的教授們。如果電機系要請全系教授一起開會的話，這個會議就稱做是 faculty meeting。大部分的學校還會有教職員餐廳（faculty lounge）供教授們吃午餐。faculty 也可以指小學和中學老師，但相形之下還是比較常指大學老師。

注意上面例句的介系詞是用 on the faculty of X department，另外我們也可以說 Professor Lin is a member of the faculty。但是 in the faculty 絕對是錯誤用法，請大家務必小心。

> **小試身手**
>
> 1. 她不是研究生，是教職員。
>
> _____

（2）in that 用以澄清前面的形容（1段）

He's a typical EE professor in that success has always come easily for him.
他是一個典型的電機系教授，從小就一切順利。

解析

筆者想像中的電機系教授應該是個男人、戴眼鏡，不常運動，大部分的時間都花在電腦上，當然也相當聰明。但是你的想像或許跟我的不一樣，所以如果我正在描述一個你從未見過的人，我說他是一個典型的電機系教授，你可能會納悶：「怎樣才算典型？」藉著使用 in that 這個用法，就能進一步闡述我的意思。同樣地，如果想要描述一個律師，可以說：

◈ She's an atypical lawyer in that she dislikes confrontation.
　她是個非典型的律師，不喜歡衝突。

這個句型並不限於用在人身上—它也可以用在描述其他事物上，如同以下小試身手所示：

小試身手

2-1. 這家公司的成功很奇特，完全不用網路行銷。

　　_____

2-2. 他是個好朋友，很忠誠，但是偶爾有點瘋狂。

　　_____

（3）smooth sailing 一帆風順（1段）

From then on, it was smooth sailing: he earned his Ph.D. just three years after his MS.

然後就一帆風順，碩士後三年，就拿到博士學位。

解析

這又是另一個英文與中文用法相同的詞彙：sail 當然是帆的意思，順則可以翻成 smooth。唯一不同的地方是，它在英文只能當名詞用，但中文用法卻是有彈性得多了。

小試身手

3. 不要以為結了婚以後你的人生就一帆風順。

　　_____

（4）wrap one's head around 搞懂（1段）

Honestly, even the hotshot professor he had for an adviser couldn't wrap his head around his dissertation.

說實話，他的指導教授雖然是一位大教授，但根本弄不清楚他的博士論文是怎麼一回事。

解析

這真是一個很難翻譯的句子！我花了一點時間才想出來要怎麼讓口語英文聽起來像是博士論文的內容過於艱澀，連聰明絕頂的教授都無法完全瞭解它。

wrap one's head around 是 e 世代的英語產物，也就是科技開始複雜到幾乎困惑每一個人的時代。想像一下，你可以把極力想瞭解的事物封在一個盒子裡。如果你想知道它的話，你必須要有足夠的「包裝紙（wrapping paper）」（也就是腦力）才能包住整個盒子。事情愈難，箱子就愈大，因此要用你的腦力去包住它就會愈顯困難。

另外一個值得一提的字是 hotshot，指的是一個人在他從事的領域中相當厲害。除了技巧卓越外，它也隱含了愛現之人的意思，特別是用在類似以下例句中：

◇ I can't wait to beat that hotshot.
　我迫不及待打敗那個自以為了不起的傢伙。

在原文例句中還隱含了嘲諷，就像中文裡的大牌：如果那位指導教授真的是個天才的話，為什麼他會不懂學生的博士論文呢？

小試身手

4-1. 你和彼得見過面嗎？他是我們新來的攝影高手。

_____

4-2. 我討厭有機化學！無論我多努力，就是讀不懂。

_____

(5) tie the knot 結婚（2段）

He and his longtime fiancée had never tied the knot.

他雖然有了未婚妻，卻好久沒有結婚。

解析

如同單字解說，knot 就是結的意思。關於結，你可以做兩件事：打結(tie it) 和解開結(untie it)。當然，世上有各式各樣的結，但是唯獨 tie the knot 才有 結婚的意思 (注意 untie the knot 並沒有離婚的意思)。

相當巧地，中文字「結」也都用在打結和結婚上，所以英文用法各位應該不 難瞭解。

Longtime 也相當值得注意，雖然它的意思相當明顯，但在中文卻沒有相對應 的形容詞。可參見以下的小試身手5-1。

小試身手

5-1. 上個禮拜我的老朋友(認識很久的朋友)比爾‧詹森過世了。

_____

5-2 去年我將近一半的朋友都結了婚。

_____

（6）drag one's feet 拖三拖四（2段）

His fiancée, it seemed, was dragging her feet: no matter how hard he tried, she refused to set a date for their wedding.

似乎他的未婚妻老是拖三拉四的，不論他如何努力，他的未婚妻始終不給他確定的結婚時間。

解析

如果你曾經帶小孩到一個他不願意去的地方的話，你應該就很能體會這個句子：這小孩不但不會自己走到那裡，如果你硬拉他的話，他還會雙腳拖地。這個用法也適用在不合作的大人身上。

既然我們提到了 feet 和 marriage，還有另一個實用片語值得一提：to get cold feet，意思是說對於承諾（譬如婚姻）臨陣退縮，特別是指最後一刻改變主意。例如：

◇ She broke off the engagement because she got cold feet.
她因臨陣退縮而中止婚約。

> **小試身手**
>
> 6. 我覺得問題在於他懶惰：每次邀他陪我去健身房，他都拖三拉四。
>
> _____

（7）if worst comes to worst 如果最糟的情形發生（5段）

He even said that if worst came to worst, he could do a DNA test to prove he had been "falsely accused" by the boy.

他還說，實在迫不得已，他可以利用 DNA 檢驗來證明他完全是被小男孩栽贓的。

解析

想像一下，你想要賭一場賽馬，但你的另一半卻因為風險太高而不表贊同。這時你要怎麼消除她/他的疑慮，讓對方知道不會有壞事發生？碰到這種狀況，你可以這麼說：

◇ Don't worry, I won't bet very much. If worst comes to worst, I won't buy that new camera lens I've been wanting.
別擔心，我不會賭太多。最糟的話，不過是不能買期待已久的新相機鏡片罷了。

come to 大致上可以翻成「變得」。假使你覺得「如果最糟變得最糟」聽起來很奇怪的話，別擔心，不是只有你這麼認為，大部分的字典也同意你的看法。有些人會說 if worse comes to worst，但還是以我列出的說法較為常見。最重要的是要記住這都是用來指「最糟的情形」。

其次，我把 falsely accused 用引號框起來是為了清楚表示林教授說話滑稽的樣子。

小試身手

7. 是沒錯，我可能不會喜歡這份工作，但它還是值得一試。即使很討厭，我辭職就算了。

　　_____

（8）on condition that（前面的結果實現的）條件是……（10段）

As expected, Professor Lin received an official letter from the DSA notifying him that he had been approved to formally adopt the boy—on condition that he married within the next three months.
果真林教授得到了一份南投縣社會局的公文，他們原則上同意林教授正式收養那個男孩子，唯一的條件的是必須在三個月內結婚。

解析

要瞭解這個用法，光知道 condition 的意思還不夠，要多注意前面的 on 以及 that，特別是 on。例如：一個假釋法官可能會對囚犯這麼說：

◇ I'll let you out of jail early on condition that you do 100 hours of community service.
我可以讓你早點離開監獄，只要你做滿100小時的社區服務。

或者老闆會這樣對新進員工說：

◇ I guarantee you a promotion within six months on condition that you come to work on time and do your job well.
只要你準時來上班並且做好你的工作，我保證你在六個月內會升官。

這個片語的前面並不需要任何的標點符號——我在原文中用的破折號是為了要戲劇化地強調後面的子句。

小試身手

小試身手

8. 只要你願意賠修車的錢，這次車禍我就不報警。

_____

（9） sweat bullets 捏一把冷汗；on one's behalf 代表；替（11段）

We all sweat bullets on Professor Lin's behalf.
我們都替林教授捏了一把冷汗。

解析

英文上也會形容緊張的人冒冷汗(sweat cold sweat)，但我覺得在這應該用別種說法會比較好。如果你 sweat bullets 的話，並不是指你被槍打中了，而是指你流了很多汗——一般而言子彈比汗滴大多了。而且通常緊張的時候才會流最多汗。

原文例句後半段 on Professor Lin's behalf 翻成中文的意思是「替林教授」，這跟 for Professor Lin「為林教授」有著些微的不一樣。Behalf 不會單獨存在，它只會跟 on 同時出現。

小試身手

9-1.你的朋友好心地替我們付了帳單。

_____

9-2.喬治在他重要的工作面試前緊張得流汗。

_____

（10）turn out（結果是）的用法（15段、21段、22段）

I always felt like that the way everything had turned out was too perfect.
總覺得這個故事發展得太過完滿。

Professor Lin turned out to be not just a good husband but a good father too.
林教授不僅僅是個好丈夫，也是個好爸爸。

Professor Lin thought that if he made up a story that thoroughly tricked his fiancée, everything would turn out wonderfully.
林教授自以為只要能編出一個將未婚妻騙得團團轉的故事，一切就很美滿。

In fact, the real reason everything had turned out so well was that he was a good man.
其實不然，他的故事發展得如此之好，是因為他是個好人。

解析

這是一個相當常見的實用動詞片語，但是因為沒有相對應的中文，所以翻譯上還蠻微妙的，而這也是為什麼在這故事裡出現了好幾個 turn out：讓你知道它可以用在不同的句型上。它的意思有點是「結果是……」的意味，但你可以發現上面原文的中文翻譯完全都沒用到「結果」二字。要瞭解這個片語的意思和用法，最好的方法就是練習。

小試身手

10-1. 今天早上看起來陰陰的，結果卻是美麗的一天。

_____

10-2. 我知道你不希望你們的關係變這樣，但是你必須面對現實。

_____

(11) consist of 由……構成 (17段)

The email I sent consisted of a single sentence.
這封電子郵件只有一句話。

解析

即使你之前已經看過這個片語，就算再多一些練習也只對你有益無害。中文翻譯相當清楚，但如同上面原文例句所示，consist of 比中文的「構成」還要能廣泛應用。

小試身手

11-1. 每個水分子有兩個氫原子和一個氧原子。

_____

11-2. 他的「論點」只有可疑的邏輯夾雜著人身攻擊。

_____

（12）**to the point** 到⋯⋯的程度（21段）

He loved to tell fibs, to the point that sometimes she had a hard time discerning whether he was telling the truth or just another tall tale.

也就是因為林教授特別會亂編故事，有的時候，她簡直弄不清楚林教授講的是故事還是事實。

解析

林教授愛說「故事」愛到什麼程度呢？愛到連他的未婚妻有時候也無法分辨什麼是「事實」，什麼是「故事」。這時候你就可以用 to the point that 這個片語來表示程度。另外舉例來說，如果你的朋友工作很拼命，拼命到沒有時間和家人、朋友相處，你可以怎樣形容他？

My friend is hardworking to the point of neglecting his friends and family.

或者

My friend is hardworking to the point that he neglects his friends and family.

當然，你也可以用 so 和 that 改寫這個句子：

My friend is so hardworking that he neglects his friends and family.

但假使你要強調的特徵比較複雜的話，用 to the point 會比較好。

小試身手

12-1. 她跑步跑到筋疲力盡為止。

_____

12-2. 他的疑心變得很重，把大家看成可能的敵人，包括他的朋友在內。

_____

（13）stretch the truth 扭曲事實（21段）

Professor Lin had a very good heart—he just liked to stretch the truth a bit.

林教授心腸非常好，只是有時有點狡猾。

解析

實際上 stretch 的意思是拉緊或拉長，而不是扭曲，扭曲比較像是 twist。人們在運動前會先伸展肌肉(stretch their muscles)暖身，或是人們會拉長衣服(stretch their clothes)讓衣服寬鬆一些。要是你拉得太過火的話，它就會破掉甚至斷掉。

並非所有的謊話都是一樣的：有一些謊話像是林教授亂編的故事，聽起來都像真的，但不是絕對真實。英文中，謊話就像浮誇的事實，意味著人們不自然地延伸事實並超出它的界限，卻又不完全偏離事實，很傳神吧？如果有人跟你說一件你覺得很誇張的事時，你就可以諷刺地說 Oh, that's a stretch。

小試身手

13-1. 她的故事說得很好聽，但你要記得她往往說得有點誇張。

_____

13-2. 這些謎題被設計來訓練你的腦力。

_____

小試身手解答

1.　She's not a student, she's a member of the faculty.

　　或 She's not a student, she's on the faculty.

2-1.　The company's success is unusual in that it has come entirely without Internet marketing.

2-2.　He's a good friend in that he's loyal, but he can be a little crazy at times.

3.　Don't assume that your life will be smooth sailing after you get married.

4-1.　Have you met Peter? He's our new hotshot photographer.

4-2.　I hate organic chemistry! No matter how hard I study, I just can't seem to wrap my head around it.

5-1.　Bill Johnson, my longtime friend, passed away last week.

5-2　Last year nearly half my friends tied the knot.

6.　I think the problem is that he's lazy: every time I ask him to go to the gym with me, he drags his feet.

7.　Sure, I may not like the job, but it's worth a try. If worst comes to worst, I'll quit.

8.　I won't report the accident to the police on condition that you pay for the damage to my car.

9-1. Your friend was kind enough to pay the bill on our behalf.

9-2. George was sweating bullets before his big job interview.

10-1. It looked cloudy this morning, but it turned out to be a beautiful day.

10-2. I know you didn't want your relationship to turn out this way, but you have to face the facts.

11-1. Every water molecule consists of two hydrogen atoms and one oxygen atom.

11-2. His "argument" consisted of questionable logic mixed with personal attacks.

12-1. She ran to the point of exhaustion.

12-2. He's gotten suspicious to the point that he sees everyone as a potential enemy, even his friends.

13-1. She's a great storyteller, but you have to remember that she tends to stretch the truth.

13-2. These puzzles are designed to stretch your brain.

The Test

考試

1-5 謹以此文獻給全國辛苦教書的中小學老師

明天，我就要退休了。

做了整整三十五年的中學老師，我可以說我這一輩子過得非常充實，非常有意義。

我到現在還記得我開始當中學老師的那一年，我一畢業，就進入了一所明星中學去教數學，學生完全是經過精挑細選選出來的，很少功課不好，我教起來當然是得心應手，輕鬆得很。隨便我怎麼出題目都考不倒他們。

可是，我忽然注意到班上有一位同學上課似乎非常心不在焉，老是對著天花板發呆。期中考，他的數學只得了十五分，太奇怪了，全班就只有他不及格，而且分數如此之差。

6-10 有一天，放學以後，我請他和我談天，這小子一問三不知，對他的成績大幅滑落，他講不出任何理由。他一再地說他上課聽不懂我講什麼，我卻覺得他不用功，因此就威脅他，說要找他的家長談談。這位

CD1-4
- ◇ primary school (n.) 小學
- ◇ secondary school (n.) 中學(國中和高中)
- ◇ decade (n.) 十年
- ◇ select (v.) 挑選
- ◇ virtually (adv.) 幾乎
- ◇ effortless (adj.) 容易的、不費吹灰之力的
- ◇ handle (v.) 處理；應付
- ◇ preoccupied (adj.) 心不在焉的
- ◇ gaze (v.) 凝視
- ◇ absently (adj.) 出神地

Dedicated to the hardworking primary and secondary school teachers of Taiwan

1-5
CD1-3

Tomorrow I'm going to retire.

Having taught high school for three and a half decades, I can say that I've led a very full and meaningful life.

I still remember my first year as a middle school teacher. Just after I graduated, I took a job as a math teacher at ultra-elite high school. All of my students had been carefully selected for their ability; virtually none of them did poor work. Naturally, I was able to teach them whatever I wanted—it was effortless. They could handle any problem I gave them.

But then I noticed that one of my students always seemed preoccupied in class, gazing absently at the ceiling. On midterm exams, he scored only 15% on math. It was bizarre—he was the only one in the class who failed, and with such an abysmal score too.

One day after school, I asked him to stay for a chat. He had no answers for my questions and couldn't come up with a reason why his grades had slipped so low. He kept saying that he didn't understand what I said in class, but in my view he wasn't trying hard enough. So I threatened to have a talk with his parents. When he heard that, he panicked. His father had got sick and died when he was only five

6-10

◈ bizarre (adj.) 詭異的；奇怪的
◈ abysmal (adj.) 極差的；糟透的
◈ slip (v.) 滑落

◈ threaten (v.) 威脅
◈ panic (v.) 驚惶失措

學生一聽到我要去找他的家長，立刻緊張了起來，他說他的父親生病去世了，當時他只有五歲，母親改嫁後到了美國，沒有帶他去，他一個人和他祖母一起住，經濟情形很好，可是他說他祖母年紀大了，連國語都不太會講，也不認識字，如果他知道了他功課不好，一定會非常傷心的。他被我逼急了，忽然問我，「老師，難道你以為我騙你？難道我會做題目，而假裝不會做？」

我被他問得啞口無言，除了鼓勵他以後上課要用功一點以外，還答應替他補習數學，而且當天晚上就開始。

這位同學一開始還老大不願意接受我做他的義務家教老師，可是由於我的堅持，他只好晚上乖乖地在我的督導之下做習題，我發現他其實不笨，只是對數學反應慢了一點，可是由於我每週替他補習二次，他終於趕上了進度，考得越來越好。二個月以後，我就不管他了。

這位學生以後就和我很親密了，當時我們夫妻兩人沒有小孩，我太太知道這孩子沒有父母以後，就找他來吃飯，他有什麼事情，一定會來找我商量，包括一些生涯規劃的問題。

他考大學也算順利，去成功嶺以前還來向我們辭行，可是第三天，

◇ plenty (n.) 足夠的量
◇ illiterate (adj.) 不識字的
◇ devastated (adj.) 極為傷心的
◇ persist (v.) 堅持
◇ blurt out (v.) 衝口說
◇ speechless (adj.) 無言

years old, he said, and his mother remarried and moved to America, leaving him behind. He lived alone with his grandma. They had plenty of money to live on, but she was very old and couldn't really speak Mandarin, and she was illiterate. If she knew he was doing poorly in school, he said, she would be devastated. I persisted until he blurted out, "Teacher, do you really think I'm lying to you? Do you really think that I know the answers but pretend not to?"

His question left me speechless. Besides encouraging him to work a little harder in class in the future, I told him I would tutor him in math, starting that evening.

At first, the boy really didn't want me as his volunteer tutor, but I insisted. And so that night he was forced to obediently work through practice problems under my direction. I discovered that he wasn't stupid, just a bit slow to pick up on mathematical concepts. Nevertheless, as I continued to tutor him twice a week, he finally caught up with the rest of the class, and his test grades rose continually. Two months later, I stopped worrying about him.

After that, this student and I became close friends. Back then, my wife and I had no children; when she found out he had no parents, she started inviting the boy over for meals. He came to me for advice about everything, including his plans for the future.

His college entrance exams went fairly smoothly, and before he left to do his military service he came to bid me farewell. Three

◇ insist (v.) 堅持
◇ obediently (adv.) 服從地
◇ concept (n.) 觀念
◇ advice (n.) 忠告；意見

我收到一封他的信，信的內容令我吃了一驚。

老師：

11-15　　請原諒我騙了你一次，當年我功課忽然一落千丈，是我故意的，我一直沒有爸爸，也想有個爸爸，這樣，如果有什麼問題，我好問問他，因此我心生一計，我發現我的英文老師，國文老師和數學老師都是男老師，我決定假裝功課不好，看看他們反應如何。

　　我的英文老師對我的成績是完全無動於衷，他將考卷還給我的時候，一點表情也沒有，我的國文老師將我臭罵一頓，他說他最痛恨不用功的學生，他罰我站了一小時，我雖然只有高一，個子已經很高，高個子最怕罰站，這麼大的人了，還要被羞辱，我當然心情不好，第二天〈赤壁賦〉一個字也背不出來，國文老師發現我交了白卷以後，立刻又罰我站，然後，在下課的時候，他向全班宣佈，他已放棄了我。

　　唯一關心我的就是你，你不但一再地問我怎麼一回事，還替我補

◇ astonished (adj.) 大驚的
◇ forgive (v.) 原諒
◇ react (v.) 反應

◇ apathetic (adj.) 不在乎的；無所謂的
◇ let loose (v.) 發飆
◇ despise (v.) 藐視；痛恨

days later, however, I received a letter from him that left me quite astonished.

Teacher,

Please forgive me for telling you a lie. When my grades fell through the floor that year, it was not an accident. I'd never had a dad before, and I wanted a dad so that if I ever had any questions, I'd have someone to come to. So I thought of a plan: since my English teacher, Chinese teacher and math teacher were all men, I decided to become a bad student in their classes and see how they would react.

My English teacher was apathetic: he handed back my test paper with a blank face. My Chinese teacher completely let loose at me: he said he despised lazy students more than anything, and he punished me by making me stand for an hour. Even though I was only a freshman, I was quite tall, and tall kids hate having to stand like that. Of course, being humiliated at that age naturally put me in a bad mood. The next day, I didn't write down a single word of "Red Cliff Rhapsody," which we were supposed to have memorized. When the teacher saw my blank paper, he immediately made me stand again. When the bell rang, he announced to the whole class that he had given up on me.

The only person who cared about me was you. Not only did you ask me what was wrong, you tutored me as well. Actually, it would

◇ humiliate (v.) 恥辱
◇ rhapsody (n.) 狂想曲；狂文 (現在漢學家一般用 rhapsody 來翻譯「賦」)

習。其實你只要關心就夠了，我完全沒有想到你免費地當我的家教老師，我必須假裝不懂，如此裝了整整兩個月之後，才脫離苦海，但我從此發現我很會演戲。

　　最使我感動的人，其實是師母，她對我的關心，令我永遠也忘不了。師母第一次請我去吃晚飯，正好寒流過境，我故意沒有穿夾克。師母一看到我衣服單薄，立刻押著我去附近的冬衣地攤，替我選了一件厚夾克，我知道老師薪水不高，還對我這麼好，我知道我找到爸爸媽媽了。

　　我從此以後將你當作我的爸爸，有什麼事，我都會問你，你也都會給我建議，我也偷偷的學你的為人處事。你對人誠懇，我也因此儘量對人誠懇，這些都是你所不知道的事。

16-20　　我要在此請你原諒我，我當年騙你，實在是迫不得已，我的確需要一個好爸爸，也虧得你對我關懷，使我從此凡事都有人可以商量。由於你在我功課不好的時候沒有放棄我，你是我一生中對我影響最大的人。

◇ suffering (n.) 受苦
◇ touch (v.) 感動
◇ front (n.) 鋒
◇ intentionally (adv.) 故意地
◇ merchant (n.) 商人
◇ stall (n.) 攤

have been enough for you to care; I never thought you would also tutor me for free. I had to pretend not to understand for two whole months before the suffering ended. But I did discover that I had a talent for acting.

But it was your wife who touched me most deeply—I will never forget the concern she showed for me. The first time she had me over for dinner, a cold front was passing through, and I intentionally showed up without a jacket. As soon as she saw my thin clothes, she marched me off to the neighborhood winter clothing merchant's stall and picked out a thick jacket for me. Teachers, I knew, didn't make much money, yet the two of you were so kind to me—I knew I had found my mom and dad.

After that, I saw you as my dad. Whenever I had anything on my mind, I came to you, and you always gave me advice. I even quietly emulated your moral character. You treated people sincerely, so I tried to treat them sincerely too. You never knew any of this.

Now I want to ask for your forgiveness. When I lied to you that year, I had no other choice. I really did need a good dad, and thanks to the love you showed for me, I will always have someone to come to for advice. Because you didn't give up on me when my grades dropped, you have had a greater influence on me than anyone else in my life.

16-20

◇ pick out (v.) 挑選
◇ emulate (v.) 效法

◇ character (n.) 品德
◇ give up (v.) 放棄(受詞前要加 on)

祝 教安

張某某上

騙你的學生

　　這封信令我出了一身冷汗，我們當老師的一天到晚考學生，我們很少想到學生也在考我們。我的那位學生出了一個考題，顯然只有我通過了這場考試。

21-24　　我從此以後就特別的注意後段班的同學，無論他們的資質如何，我都不輕言放棄，我總會儘量地幫助他們，使他們能學多少就學多少。這麼多年來，我教了不知道多少功課不好的同學，有幾位大器晚成，還得到了博士學位，不論他們的學業成就如何，他們都在社會上有工作可做，沒有一位出問題的。

　　我發現後段班同學雖然成就不見得好，卻非常感激我，他們的任何成就，不論大小，都令我感到驕傲。

　　明天，有很多我過去教過的學生來參加我的退休茶會，大多數恐怕都是當年的後段班同學，那位騙我的同學當然一定會來，他的事業很

◇ regardless (adv.) 不論　　　　◇ write off (v.) 放棄
◇ aptitude (n.) 天資　　　　　　◇ late bloomer (n.) 大器晚成的人

Happy teaching,

Zhang

The student who lied to you

By the time I finished the letter, I had broken out in a cold sweat. As teachers, we're constantly testing our students, yet we seldom realize that our students test us as well. My student had come up with a test question, and apparently I was the only one who passed.

After that, I always paid special attention to the bottom half of my students. Regardless of their level of aptitude, I refused to write them off—I always did my best to help them learn as much as they could. Over the long course of my career, I've taught countless poorly performing students. A few of them have been late bloomers, going on to get Ph.D.s. But whatever their level of academic success, all of them have good jobs, and none of them have gotten into trouble. **21-24**

I've found that though their grades may not be good, the students in the bottom half really appreciate what I do. Every one of their achievements, no matter how big or small, makes me proud.

Tomorrow, many of my former students will come to my retirement reception. Most of them, I bet, will be the ones from the bottom half. Of course, the student who lied to me that first year will be there. He's

◈ achievement (n.) 成就
◈ reception (n.) 招待會

◈ bet (v.) 打賭：這裡指「猜」

成功，一直和我保持密切的聯絡。我要在明天告訴他，我才應該謝謝他，他改變了我的一生，他是我一生中對我影響最大的人。

had a very successful career and has kept in close touch with me. Tomorrow I will tell him that I'm the one who should thank him. He changed my life. He has had a greater influence on me than anyone else in my life.

(1) 文法概念：having＋過去分詞（2段）

Having taught in high school for three and a half decades, I can say that I've led a very full and meaningful life.

做了整整三十五年的中學老師，我可以說我這一輩子過得非常充實，非常有意義。

解析

這個句子的中英文組織大致相同，因此即使你不懂文法規則，也能輕易地猜出它的意思。

回想一下，過去分詞通常用於表示從以前開始持續至今的動作，或是之前開始到最近才剛完成的動作。例如：

◈ I have felt tired all day.
我整天都覺得累。

◈ We have finished the job.
我們已把工作做完了。

倘若我們要把整個完成式動詞片語移到句首，而將主詞留在後面的話，這時候該怎麼做呢？其實只要把 have/has 變成 having 就可以了。如果要把例句原文改寫成主詞在前的句子，它就會變成這樣：

I have taught high school for three and a half decades, so I can say that I've led a very full and meaningful life.

這是正確的句子，但是卻會讓人覺得無趣，主詞 "I" 重覆了兩次也讓人覺得嘮叨。

這個句子另外值得一提的是動詞 led（lead 過去式）與 life 之間的用法。或許從中文的角度看來會覺得很奇怪，因為中文沒有相對應的說法。可能當初創造這個說法的人想要告訴世人命運操之在己，強調人們應該導引而非跟從我們的宿命吧。

> **小試身手**
>
> 1-1. 環遊了世界，我發現真的是金窩銀窩都不如自己的狗窩。
>
> _____
>
> 1-2. 她此生過得很精彩，死而無憾。
>
> _____

（2）come up with 想出；找出（6段、20段）

He had no answers for my questions and couldn't come up with a reason why his grades had slipped so low.

這小子一問三不知，對他的成績大幅滑落，他講不出任何理由。

My student had come up with a test question.

我的那位學生出了一個考題。

解析

台灣的電視新聞總愛報導無助的窮人向地下錢莊借錢，最後還不出錢走投無路的新聞。那些高利貸會用盡各種威脅手段好收回帳款，他們不在乎錢是怎麼來的，只要債務人想出辦法找出（come up with）錢來就好。

同樣地，故事裡這位老師的學生想必會編出無數個藉口來解釋他的爛成績，但他就是想不出確切的原因。而這個學生出給老師的「考題」是從他腦中的某個地方想出來的，至於確切位置，沒人知道。

小試身手

2-1. 科學家想出了從海水提取(extract)飲用水的新方法。

_____

2-2. 我們需要想出一個吸引高齡消費者的新產品

_____

（3）leave＋sb＋情緒形容詞 令某人……；讓某人感到……(9段)

Three days later, however, I received a letter from him that left me quite astonished.

可是第三天，我收到一封他的信，信的內容令我大吃一驚。

解析

一般而言，生活都是一成不變的：早上吃早餐，工作到傍晚，晚上有幾小時休閒時間，然後第二天又繼續重覆同樣的一天。但是每隔一陣子總有一些出乎意料的事發生，打亂了我們的計畫。這時，我們要如何反應？這就要取決於這個驚喜是讓我們愉悅、生氣、沮喪或快樂了。這個用法就像若有朋友驟逝，即便已不在人世，可是留下來的感覺卻不會那麼快就消失。這也就是為什麼英文用 leave 這個字來形容這種感覺。以下兩個例子可以說明我的意思：

◈ The way she criticized me behind my back left me feeling betrayed.
她那樣背後批評我，讓我覺得自己被背叛。

◈ My boss's unexpected compliment left me wondering what I had done to make her so happy.
老闆突如其來的稱讚讓我納悶自己倒底是做了什麼事讓她這麼開心。

小試身手

3-1. 他退休的消息讓我們啞口無言。

_____

3-2. 他太太的驟逝留下他一個人孤獨心碎。

_____

（4）do/did 用以強調動詞（13段、16段）

But I did discover that I had a talent for acting.
但我從此發現我很會演戲。

I really did need a good dad.
我的確需要一個好爸爸。

解析

do/did 除了一般用法外，它也能用來強調後面接著的動詞。在第一個原文例句中，這個學生寫出了整整兩個月都要假裝不懂數學是多麼無聊的一件事。但這並不全然都是損失，他說至少他發現他還蠻會演戲的。句中的 did 就是用來強調這份在負面情勢中找尋正面力量的努力。

第二個句子就更簡單了。為了解釋他撒謊的原因，這個學生強調了他渴望擁有父親的心意是真切的。did 就是強調這個需求的真實性。因此，第一個句子的 did 可以翻成「至少」或「起碼」，第二個句子就可以翻成「的確」。

> **小試身手**
>
> 4-1. 或許你不用買花，但是我認為你還是應該道歉。
>
> _____
>
> 4-2. 甲：她為什麼沒有警告我？
>
> 　　乙：她有警告你，但是你沒有聽。
>
> _____
>
> _____

（5）have something on one's mind 有心事；有話要說；在想某件事（15段）

Whenever I had anything on my mind, I came to you, and you always gave me advice.

有什麼事，我都會問你，你也都會給我建議。

解析

當我們做事的時候，我們會把東西放在桌上好便於取用。同樣地，當一個人在想事情、煩惱的時候，事情就會如烏雲罩頂般 on your mind。通常這個片語都用在如果情況允許之下你想要跟朋友討論的事。例如：

◇ You look like you've got something on your mind. Do you want to talk?
　你看起來好像在想什麼心事，要不要說說看？

切記不要把 in 和 on 搞混了。in one's mind 的用法完全不同，它只是一個在心裡短暫的想法，一個尚未現實的念頭：I think the problem is in your mind.（我覺得問題只存在於你的心裡。）

5. 她總是看起來壓力很大，好像有什麼事情困擾著她。

_____

（6）as 身為；作為（20段）

As teachers, we're constantly testing our students, yet we seldom realize that our students test us as well.

我們當老師的一天到晚考學生，我們很少想到學生也在考我們。

解析

當我們想要強調一個人的職位或角色的話，我們就可以使用這個用法，例如：

◇ As your doctor, I feel professionally obligated to urge you to exercise more.

身為你的醫生，我覺得有職業上的義務勸你多運動。

◇ I saw my teacher in the supermarket yesterday. It was weird—I'm not used to seeing him as a regular person.

昨天我在超市看到了我的老師，感覺很奇怪，我不習慣把他當普通人看。

6. 身為員警的女兒，我看不慣輕視員警的人。

_____

（7）bet 打賭；猜想（23段）

Most of them, I bet, will be the ones from the bottom half.
大多數恐怕都是當年的後段班同學。

解析

如果你喜歡賭博的話，你就能瞭解這個字。賭博就是猜測：你不知道結果如何，但是你相信自己的直覺，打賭(bet)押注在你認為會發生的事。基於這個不確定因素，bet 這個字也常會用來猜測與賭博無關的事。其他類似的字還有 suppose, imagine 和 predict。

◈ I imagine the weather where you live is pretty cold this time of year.
　我想你那邊的天氣這時候應該很冷吧。

◈ Who do you suppose/predict will win the game tonight?
　你覺得今天晚上的球賽誰會贏？

這些字在字義上有著些微的差異，下次聽到英語母語人士說到這些字的時候可以多注意它的用法。但是，注意只有 bet 這個字才能用在賭博上喔。

小試身手

7-1. 那個考試好難啊！我應該是班上成績最差的吧。

_____

7-2. 他預測油價會在這五年內加倍。

_____

7-3. 我猜洋基隊今年會進季後賽吧。

_____

小試身手解答

1-1. Having traveled around the world, I discovered that there really is no place like home.

1-2. She led an exciting life and died with no regrets.

2-1. Scientists have come up with a new way to extract drinking water from seawater.

2-2. We need to come up with a new product that will appeal to older consumers.

3-1. The news of his retirement left us speechless.

3-2. His wife's sudden death left him alone and heartbroken.

4-1. You might not need to buy flowers, but I do think that you should apologize.

4-2. A: Why didn't she warn me?

B: She did warn you, but you didn't listen.

5. She always looks stressed out, like she has something on her mind.

6. As the daughter of a police officer, I'm offended by people who don't respect the police.

7-1. That exam was so hard! I bet I got the worst grade in the class.

7-2. He predicted that the price of oil would double in the next five years. (一定要用 predict，因為這不只是猜，是預測。)

7-3. I bet the Yankees will make the playoffs this year.

The Great Author's Dream
大作家的夢想

1-5　　大作家是個天才，小學的時候，天才就展現出來了，無論老師出什麼題目，他都能毫無困難地寫出一篇極有創意的作文。有一次，老師出了一個有關醫生的題目，別的孩子都死板板地談醫生如何偉大，如何有愛心，如何替人類減少了痛苦。我們的大作家卻寫了一個有趣的故事，故事中，醫生自己變成了病人，由於他的醫生知識，他知道他的病情多嚴重，幾乎無藥可救，到了這一時刻，他忽然非常後悔他是個優秀的醫生。如果他不知道他的病無藥可治，他一定會過得比較快樂。當時，大作家只是個國中生。

　　可是，大作家也有一次滑鐵盧的經驗，他參加進大學的考試，發現作文題目是「一個窮人的日記」。大作家忽然寫不出來了，他知道世界上有窮人，可是他一時無法想像窮人如何思想的，因為他出身於一個富有的家庭，有生之年，他沒有碰到過一個窮人。最後，他胡亂寫了一些，交了卷。

　　雖然大作家的作品都非常精彩，他永遠沒有忘掉他的這個難題，這是他一生中唯一寫不出來的文章，他對這件事耿耿於懷，總想有一天他能寫出一篇代表窮人心聲的文章，而且他希望這篇文章能永垂不朽。

CD1-6

◇ evident (adj.) 明顯的
◇ assign (v.) 出(功課)
◇ compose (v.) 創造
◇ remarkably (adv.) 非常；顯著地
◇ formulaic (adj.) 公式化、制式的
◇ charitable (adj.) 博愛的(charity 的形容詞)
◇ incurable (adj.) 不可醫治的

The great author was a genius, and his gift was evident from his elementary school days: no matter what subject the teacher assigned, he could compose a remarkably creative essay on it without difficulty. Once, when a teacher chose doctors as the topic, the other children wrote the usual formulaic stuff about how great and charitable doctors are and how they ease the pain of mankind, but our great author penned an interesting story in which a doctor became a patient, and because of his medical training, he knew how serious his illness was—virtually incurable. At that moment he suddenly regretted being an eminent physician, for had he not known that his disease was incurable, he would have been happier. The great author was only a middle school student at the time.

But even the great author met his Waterloo. When he took his college entrance exams, the topic for the essay was "A Poor Man's Diary." All of a sudden he found himself unable to write. He knew there were poor people in the world, but he couldn't imagine what they thought about, for he had been born into a rich family and had never met a poor man before. He ended up scribbling down whatever he could and handing it in.

Although all of the great author's stories were terrific reads, he never forgot the topic that had defeated him. It was the only essay he had ever been unable to write in his life, and he took it deeply to heart, hoping that someday he would be able to write a piece that spoke for the poor and would stand the test of time.

◈ eminent (adj.) 出類拔萃的
◈ physician (n.) 醫生
◈ scribble (v.) 胡亂寫
◈ hand in (v.) 交 (功課等)
◈ piece (n.) 作品
◈ stand (v.) 經得起

戰爭爆發了，大作家被徵入伍。有一天，他和兩位弟兄出去巡邏，被敵人發現了，兩位伙伴都被擊斃，大作家落荒而逃，雖然擺脫了敵人，卻也迷了路，入夜以後，大作家一個不小心，掉入了很深的山谷，也昏迷了過去。

醒來以後，他發現他的兩條腿都斷了，他的槍也不見了，他設法大叫了幾次，都沒有人聽見，他靠少許乾糧和極為少量的水過了兩天。到了第四天，他已極為虛弱，當夜晚來臨的時候，他感到他可能看不到第二天的天亮了。

6-10　　可是，忽然之間，大作家發現他衣服裡還有一個火柴盒，他打開了火柴盒，看到三根火柴。擦亮了第一根火柴，他看到一個士兵平時帶的乾糧盒。擦亮了第二根火柴，他看到一個士兵平時帶的水壺。擦亮了第三根火柴，他看到一個陌生人在他的旁邊，握住了他的手。

最後一根火柴熄滅了以後，大作家知道他一生的夢想即將實現，因為他終於瞭解窮人在想些什麼：他們無非想要一些可以吃的東西、可以喝的水以及來自別人關懷。

◇ break out (v.) 爆發
◇ conscript (v.) 徵（兵）
◇ patrol (v.) 巡邏
◇ fellow (adj.) 和自己身分一樣的
◇ spot (v.) 看清楚（目標）
◇ flee (v.) 逃跑
◇ slip (v.) 失足
◇ ravine (n.) 壑

War broke out, and the great author was conscripted into the army. One day, he was out patrolling with two of his fellow soldiers when they were spotted by the enemy. His companions were shot dead, and the great author fled for his life. Though he succeeded in escaping from the enemy, he lost his way. Night fell, and the great author slipped and fell into a deep ravine, knocking himself unconscious.

When he awoke, both his legs were broken and his rifle was gone. He found the strength to call for help a few times, but nobody heard him. Relying on what little food and water he had, he subsisted for two days. By the fourth day, though, he had grown extremely weak, and when the night came, he sensed that he might not live to see the next morning.

But all of a sudden the great author discovered a small matchbox inside his uniform. He opened the matchbox and saw three matches. When he lit the first one, he saw an ordinary soldier's ration container. When he lit the second, he saw an ordinary soldier's canteen. When he lit the third match, he saw a stranger beside him, holding his hand.

6-10

As the last match went out, the great author knew that his life's dream was about to come true, for he finally understood the thoughts of the poor: all they really want is food to eat, water to drink, and someone to care about them.

◈ knock (v.) 撞擊
◈ unconscious (adj.) 不省人事的
◈ subsist (v.) 維持(生活)下去
◈ sense (v.) 感到

◈ ration (n.) 軍用口糧
◈ canteen (n.) (士兵的)水壺
◈ go out (v.) 熄滅
◈ come true (v.) 實現

　　大作家下定決心要保持清醒，直到天亮，他還有一張紙和一枝筆，他要在他臨死以前，寫一個有關窮人的故事，而且他有把握他的故事會永垂不朽。

　　大作家的屍體被人找到，人們在他的衣服裡找到了一張紙，由於他當時已經很虛弱，紙上的故事非常短。

　　大作家的故事就是〈賣火柴的小女孩〉，而且被收入《安徒生童話集》，成為家喻戶曉的小說。

◇ sheet (n.) 張；薄片　　　　　　　　◇ lay (v.) lie (躺)的過去式

The great author resolved to stay awake until dawn; he still had a sheet of paper and a pen. As he lay dying, he would write a story about the poor, a story he knew would stand the test of time.

When the great author's body was found, someone discovered a piece of paper inside his clothes. Because he had had so little strength left, the story written there was very short.

The great author's story was called *The Little Match Girl*, and it was included in Hans Christian Andersen's collection of fairy tales, becoming known and loved by nearly every household.

◇ collection (n.) 集　　　　　◇ household (n.) 家庭

（1）no matter 無論（1段）

without difficulty 沒有困難地（1段）

No matter what subject the teacher assigned, he could compose a remarkably creative essay on it without difficulty.

無論老師出什麼題目，他都能毫無困難地寫出一篇極有創意的作文。

【解析】

matter 可以當作名詞或動詞，在這個句型中，這兩種說法都通。no matter 通常後面都是接疑問詞（如 who, what, where, when, which, how）為首的子句，而這個子句可長又複雜也可短。例如：

◈ A person's a person, no matter how small.
不論個頭大小，生命就是生命。

◈ No matter which proposal you choose to adopt, you'll have my full support.
不管你採用哪個提案，我都會全力支持你。

no matter 並不一定要放在句首。另外還值得注意的是原文句尾的 without difficulty。從中文翻回來的話，補語前面應該需要像 difficultlessly 這樣的字，但是英文裡卻沒這個字。最相近的類似語是 effortlessly，然而為了不要讓整個句子因過多副詞而顯得複雜，而改用簡單的 without difficulty 加在句尾。

> **小試身手**
>
> 1-1. 無論她到哪裡，她帶著相機一起去。
>
> _____
>
> 1-2. 無論發生什麼事，朋友一定會照顧彼此。
>
> _____

(2) 文法概念：had＋主詞＋動詞＝如果（1段）

Had he not known that his disease was incurable, he would have been happier.

如果他不知道他的病無藥可治，他一定會過得比較快樂。

解析

我們先從兩個敘述句來看：那個醫生知道他的病無藥可治。這讓他不快樂。我們要怎麼把這兩個句子結合在一起呢？用 if：If he had not known that his disease was incurable, he would have been happier. 這個句子改變了動詞的形式，也就是：條件句的動詞改成過去完成式，結果子句則用 would have。關於假設句的用法在前幾冊都有詳細說明。但是如果你想要組織一個類似的句子卻不想用 if 的話，這時該怎麼做呢？只要把 had 移到主詞 he 的前面，然後把 if 刪掉就完成了。改變的文字順序正是條件句的象徵，它就像是在問問題，但是是用 had 而不是用 did。

這裡有另一個例子可供練習，假如我們想把這個句子變成條件句：

◇ She made that critical mistake, so she lost the game.

我們可以說

◇ If she hadn't made that critical mistake, she wouldn't have lost the game.

或者不用 if：

◇ Had she not made that critical mistake, she wouldn't have lost the game.

如果她沒有犯這致命的錯誤，她也不會輸掉這場比賽。

小試身手

2-1. It rained this morning.＋I brought my umbrella to work.

_____

2-2. She didn't apologize.＋He's still mad at her.

_____

（3）a terrific read 一個精彩的故事（3段）

Although all of the great author's stories were terrific reads, he never forgot the topic that had defeated him.

雖然大作家的作品都非常精彩，他永遠沒有忘掉他的這個難題。

解析

如果食物很美味的話，在中文你可以説「好吃」；如果某人有一副好嗓音的話，你會説他聲音「好聽」。在英文中也有類似的片語：如果一本書很有趣的話，有時候我們會説 it's a good read（好讀）。不巧地，中文的「精采」在英文中沒有對應的字眼，terrific read 是最貼切的説法。

小試身手

3. 如果你要找讀起來輕鬆愉快的東西，你應該看看他的書。

_____

（4）take something to heart 耿耿於懷（3段）
　　　stand the test of time 永垂不朽（經得起時間的考驗）（3段）

It was the only essay he had ever been unable to write in his life, and he took it deeply to heart, hoping that someday he would be able to write a piece that spoke for the poor and would stand the test of time.

這是他一生中唯一寫不出來的文章，他對這件事耿耿於懷，總想有一天他能寫出一篇代表窮人心聲的文章，而且他希望這篇文章能永垂不朽。

[解析]

這裡有兩個相當實用，可以直譯成英文的慣用語。大部分的人會放下自己的失敗，不讓自己老是想著(dwel on)過錯，但偶爾還是會有一兩個失敗讓人心煩。這種情形我們會説人們 take it to heart，直接帶到心坎裡。這個片語不只可以用在失敗上，在任何你想用「耿耿於懷」這個詞的時候，你大概就能用 take it to hear。副詞 deeply 只是額外強調，並非必要。例如：

◇ If you don't respect him, you shouldn't take his criticisms to heart.
　如果你不尊敬他，你就不該把他的批評放在心上。

至於 stand the test of time，首先得先瞭解 stand 和 test 還有其他的意思。Stand(經得起)，引申自在戰場上倖免於難：如果戰爭結束時，你還站著的話，你一定很厲害。而順著台灣教育體系長大的人應該都能體會為什麼 test 也有考驗的意思了。

小試身手

4-1. 一天到晚聽那麼吵的音樂，你怎麼受得了？

_____

4-2. 你無法控制的，不要耿耿於懷。

_____

4-3. 跑馬拉松是耐力的考驗。

_____

 小試身手解答

1-1. No matter where she goes, she takes her camera with her.

1-2. Friends take care of each other no matter what happens.

2-1. Had it not rained this morning, I wouldn't have brought my umbrella to work.

2-2. Had she apologized, he wouldn't still be mad at her.

3. If you're looking for a nice, easy read, you should try one of his books.

4-1. How can you stand to listen to that loud music all day long?

4-2. If you can't control it, don't take it to heart.

4-3. Running a marathon is a test of endurance.

Hard Labor
苦工

1-5　　我做大學教授已經很多年了，我注意到大學男生屬於白面書生的已經是非常少了，大多數男生都有很健康的膚色，可是比起在外面做工的工人來說，似乎我們的大學生仍然白得多了。

　　張炳漢是少數皮膚非常黑的那種大學生，難怪他的外號叫作「小黑」，我是他的導師，第一天導師生面談，他就解釋給我聽為何他如此之黑，他說他從高二開始就去工地做小工，再加上他是屏東鄉下長大的，所以皮膚黑得不得了。他說他家不富有，學費和生活費都要靠哥哥，而他哥哥就是一位完全靠勞力賺錢的建築工人，他大一暑假就跟著他哥哥打工，賺了幾萬元。

　　有一天，一位屏東縣社會局的社工人員來找我，他告訴我一件令我大吃一驚的事，他說張炳漢的父母絕不可能是他的親生父母，因為他們血型都是 O 型，而張炳漢卻是 A 型，他們早就發現了這個個案，經過電腦資料庫不斷的搜尋，他們總算找到了他的親生父母。長話短說，我只在這裡說一個強有力的證據：他們發現張炳漢其實是走失的孩子，他現在的父母領養了他，而他被發現時穿的衣服也有很清楚的

CD1-8

◇ pasty (adj.) 漿糊色的
◇ bookworm (n.) 書蟲；書呆子
◇ laborer (n.) 想想：labor＝勞動
◇ Darkie (n.) 「小黑」(注意：有些黑人會介意這種字言，覺得它有種族歧視的味道)
◇ adviser (n.) 想想：advise＝勸告；指導

◇ construction (n.) 建設
◇ junior year (n.) 高中二年級(美國某些地方的高中有四年級，和大學一樣，分別為 freshman/sophomore/junior/senior year；只有三年級的高中就沒有 freshmen)
◇ rely on (v.) 依靠

1-5
CD1-7

I've been a college professor for quite a few years. Nowadays, hardly any college boys are pasty white-skinned bookworms, I've noticed—most of them have healthy color, though they still seem far whiter than laborers who work outdoors.

Zhang Binghan was one of the few really dark-skinned college boys—it was no wonder he was nicknamed Darkie. I was his adviser. During our first interview, he explained to me why he was so dark. He had started doing construction work in his junior year of high school, and since he grew up in rural Pingtung, his skin was as dark as could be. He said his family was not rich—he relied on his older brother for tuition and living expenses. His brother was a construction worker who earned his living by the sweat of his brow. The summer after his first year of college, he worked with his brother and made tens of thousands of Taiwan dollars.

One day, a social worker from the Pingtung Social Affairs Bureau came to see me. What he told me gave me quite a shock: Zhang Binghan's mother and father couldn't possibly be his real parents because they had Type O blood, whereas Zhang Binghan's blood was Type A. They had discovered this some time ago, and after much searching through their database, they had finally found his real parents. To make a long story short, I'll only mention one particularly convincing piece of evidence: they discovered that Zhang Binghan

---

◈ tuition (n.) 學費
◈ expense (n.) 費用（往往用複數）
◈ brow (n.) 眉；額頭
◈ affair (n.) 事情；事務（常用複數）
◈ whereas (conj.) 而（用於對比）

◈ database (n.) 資料庫
◈ mention (v.) 提到
◈ convincing (adj.) 想想：convince＝說服
◈ evidence (n.) 證據

記錄，當時他只有兩歲，十八年來，他的親生父母仍保留著當年尋人的廣告，也從未放棄過找他的意念，那個廣告上的衣服和小黑當年被找到的完全吻合，再加上其他的證據，他們已可百分之百地確定小黑可以回到親生父母懷抱了。

社工人員問我小黑是一個什麼樣的孩子，我告訴他小黑性格非常爽朗，他建議我們就立刻告訴他這個消息。

小黑聽到了這個消息，當然感到十分地激動，可是，他告訴我，他早就知道他的父母不可能是他的親生父母，血型是一個因素，另一個因素是他和他哥哥完全不像，他哥哥不太會唸書，國中畢業以後就去做工了，他卻對唸書一點困難也沒有，他哥哥體格也比他強壯得多。他們倆唯一相同之處是口音，可是他認為這是因為他從小學他哥哥的緣故。

6-10　　不要看小黑年紀輕輕，他的決定卻充滿了智慧，他說他不知道他的親生父母是什麼人物，可是不論他們是什麼人，他的身份證上父母欄

◇ adopt (v.) 收養
◇ identity (n.) 身分
◇ ad (n.) 廣告 advertisement 的常用縮寫
◇ affect (v.) 影響
◇ physique (n.) 體格
◇ similarity (n.) 相似點

had gotten lost as a child, and his current parents had adopted him. The clothing he had on when he was found clearly proved his identity. He was only two years old at the time. For 18 years, his birth parents had kept a copy of their original missing person ad, and they never gave up hope of finding him. The clothes in the ad and the clothes Binghan had been found in matched perfectly. That, along with other evidence, proved beyond doubt that Darkie could return to his birth parents' embrace.

The social worker asked me what kind of boy Darkie was. I told him he was a real straight shooter. He suggested that we tell him immediately.

Needless to say, Darkie was deeply affected by the news. However, he told me he had known for a long time that his parents were not his real parents. His blood type was one reason; another was that he and his brother were totally different. Never much of a student, his brother started working as soon as he graduated from middle school. He himself, on the other hand, never had a problem with schoolwork. His brother also had a much stronger physique. Their only similarity was the way they talked, but that, he reasoned, was only because he had imitated his brother growing up.

In spite of his youth, Darkie made a very wise decision. He didn't know what kind of people his birth parents were, he said, but no matter who they were, he would not change the "Parents" field on his

6-10

◇ reason (v.) 推理
◇ imitate (v.) 模仿；學

◇ field (n.) (表上的)格

不會改變，他的理由非常簡單：他們對我這麼好，收養了我，含辛茹苦地將我帶大，我這一輩子都會認他們為爸爸媽媽。至於親生父母，我會孝順他們，將他們看成自己的父母，只是在法律上，我不要認祖歸宗了。

我和社工人員都為小黑的決定深受感動，社工人員告訴小黑，他的生父是一位地位不小的公務員，生母是中學老師，他們還有一個兒子，比小黑小一歲，念大學一年級，他們住在台北。

小黑表現得出奇鎮靜，他要和社工人員一起回屏東去，將這一切告訴他的爸爸媽媽，他的爸爸媽媽是典型的鄉下好人，他們聽到這個好消息立刻和臺北方面聯絡，約好週六小黑去台北見他的親生父母。

誰陪他去呢？這個責任落到我和太太身上，我們夫婦兩人抓了小黑，到街上去買了新的牛仔褲，新的花襯衫，當時已冷了，我們順便又替他買了一件新毛衣，星期六一早就從台中開車去台北「相親」。

◇ ID（n.）identity 或 identification 的常用縮寫
◇ take in（v.）收留
◇ endure（v.）忍受
◇ hardship（n.）考驗；困難
◇ esteem（v.）尊重
◇ rejoin（v.）重返；返回
◇ moved（adj.）感動

ID card. His reason was simple: "They've been so good to me," he said. "They took me in and endured every hardship to raise me. I'll call them Mom and Dad as long as I live. As for my birth parents, I'll respect and obey them and esteem them as my parents, only I won't legally rejoin their family."

Both the social worker and I were deeply moved by Darkie's decision. The social worker informed Darkie that his birth father was a fairly high-ranking government official, and his mother was a middle school teacher. They had another son as well, a year younger than Darkie, who was a freshman in college. They lived in Taipei.

Displaying remarkable composure, Darkie asked the social worker to accompany him to Pingtung so he could tell all this to his mom and dad. His parents were the classic rural good samaritan type. When they heard the good news, they immediately got in touch with the Taipei family and arranged for Darkie to meet his birth parents on Saturday in Taipei.

Who would go with him? The responsibility fell on me and my wife. The two of us took Darkie out to buy a new pair of jeans and a pattern shirt. Since it was cold, we bought him a new sweater too. Then, first thing Saturday morning, we drove from Taichung to Taipei to "meet the parents."

◈ fairly（adv.）頗；相當
◈ high-ranking（adj.）地位高的
◈ remarkable（adj.）出奇的；值得注意的
◈ composure（n.）鎮靜

◈ good samaritan（adj.）好心的
◈ arrange（v.）安排
◈ fall on（v.）落在

　　小黑雖然是個壯漢，可是當他走下汽車的時候，兩腿都有點軟了，幾乎由我和太太扶著他進電梯上樓，大門打開，小黑的媽媽將他一把抱住，哭得像個淚人兒，小黑有沒有掉眼淚，我已不記得了，我發現小黑比他媽媽高一個頭，現在是由他來輕拍安慰媽媽。事後，他告訴我，當天他在回台中的火車上，大哭一場，弄得旁邊的人莫名其妙。我和我太太當然識相地只坐了半小時就走了，半小時內，我觀察到他的親生父母都是非常入情入理的人，他的弟弟和他很像，可是白得多，和小黑一比，真是所謂的白面書生了。我心中暗自得意，覺得還是我們的小黑比較漂亮，尤其他笑的時候，黝黑的臉上露出一口白白的牙齒，有一種特別男孩子的魅力。

11-15　　小黑收到了件夾克做為禮物，是滑雪的那種羽毛衣，小黑當場試穿，完全合身，這也靠我事先通風報信，將小黑的尺寸告訴了他的親生父母。我的工作還沒有結束，小黑要我請客，將他的「雙方家長」都請到台中來，我這個導師只好聽命，除了兩對爸媽以外，我還請了小黑的哥哥和他的親弟弟，因為大家都是很真誠的人，宴會進行得十

◇ muscular (adj.) 肌肉發達的
◇ lean on (v.) 倚靠
◇ shed (v.) 留下(動詞三態 shed、shed、shed)
◇ pat (v.) 輕拍

◇ profusely (adv.) 豐富地(通常指強烈情感的表現)
◇ bewilderment (n.) 困惑；莫名其妙
◇ tact (n.) 識趣
◇ conceal (v.) 隱藏

Although Darkie was a muscular kid, when he got out of the car he was a little weak at the knees. He practically had to lean on me and my wife to get to the elevator. When the door opened, Darkie's mother threw her arms around him, crying like a baby. I can't remember if Darkie shed tears or not. I discovered that Darkie, now a head taller than his mother, had to pat and comfort her. He later told me that he had cried profusely on the train back to Taichung, much to the bewilderment of the people beside him. Of course, my wife and I had the tact to only stay for half an hour. During those thirty minutes, I observed that his birth parents were very sensible people, and his brother was very like him, only much lighter-skinned— compared with Darkie, he really was a pasty white-faced bookworm. Our Darkie is the handsomer of the two, I thought with concealed pleasure, especially when he laughs, revealing a mouthful of white teeth offset by his swarthy face—he has a sort of young man's special allure.

Darkie was given a jacket—one of those down-filled ski jackets— as a gift. He tried it on, and it was a perfect fit, because I had taken the liberty of telling Darkie's parents his size beforehand. My work was still not finished: Darkie wanted me to host both his families for dinner in Taichung. As his adviser, I had no choice but to obey. In addition to both sets of parents, I invited his older brother and his blood-related younger brother. They were all very genuine people,

11-15

◇ offset（v.）襯托；抵銷（注意原形動詞、過去式及過去分詞及皆同，像 set 一樣）

◇ swarthy（adj.）黝黑的（這個字也往往帶有歧視黑人的味道，要小心用）

◇ down（n.）羽絨

◇ beforehand（adv.）事先（和 afterward 相對）

◇ host（v.）做東招待

◇ genuine（adj.）真誠的

分愉快，我發現小黑的哥哥的確比他壯得多，我又發現小黑的弟弟比他白了太多，小黑好像感到這一點，他說他還有一個綽號，叫做「非洲小白臉」，他顯然希望由此說法來縮短他和弟弟間的距離。

小黑的帳戶中增加了很多錢，可是小黑的生活一如往常，只是週末有時北上臺北，有時南下屏東，他的親生母親一開始每天打電話來噓寒問暖，他只好求饒，因為同學們已經開始嘲笑他了。

大二暑假開始，小黑向我辭行，我問他暑假中要做什麼？他說他要去做苦工，我暗示他可以不必擔心學費和生活費了，他說他一定要再去屏東，和他哥哥在一起做一個暑假的苦工，他要讓他哥哥知道他沒有變，他仍是他的弟弟。

我知道屏東的太陽毒得厲害，在烈日之下抬磚頭、搬水泥，不是什麼舒服的事，我有點捨不得他做這種苦工。小黑看出了我的表情，安慰我，叫我不要擔心，他說他就是喜歡做苦工，他還告訴我他做工的時候，向來打赤膊打赤腳，這是他最痛快的時候。

◇ preppy（n/adj.）（美國的俚語）造型像讀高級私立學校的學生：穿名牌衣服，很在乎外表，通常有白皮膚
◇ beg for（v.）乞求
◇ mercy（n.）慈悲
◇ make fun of（v.）嘲笑

and the dinner was a delight. Once again I noticed how Darkie's older brother was more muscular than he and how much whiter Darkie's little brother was than the rest of them. Darkie noticed it too—he said people called him "African preppy," obviously hoping that this would shorten the distance between them.

A lot of money was added to Darkie's bank account, but his lifestyle stayed the same, except that now he occasionally went up to Taipei or down to Pingtung on weekends. At first, his birth mother called every day to check on him, until he had to beg her for mercy because his classmates were making fun of him.

When his sophomore year ended and summer vacation arrived, Darkie came to say goodbye. When I asked what his summer plans were, he told me that he was going to do construction work. I hinted that he didn't have to worry about tuition and living expenses anymore. But he insisted on going back to Pingtung and doing a summer's worth of hard labor with his brother. He wanted him to know that he hadn't changed—he was still his little bro.

I knew how harsh the Pingtung sun could be—lifting bricks and moving cement under its blazing heat was not pleasant work, and I was a bit unwilling to see him do it. Seeing the look on my face, Darkie tried to console me. He urged me not to worry—he liked doing hard labor. In fact, he said that whenever he worked, he went shirtless and barefoot, and it gave him more pleasure than anything.

◈ insist on (v.) 堅持要
◈ bro (n.) 即 brother 的親暱稱呼
◈ blazing (adj.) 炙熱的
◈ console (v.) 安慰

16-21　　可是小黑沒有騙得了我，我知道小黑不是為喜歡打赤膊、打赤腳而去做苦工的，如果僅僅只要享受這種樂趣，去游泳就可以了，我知道他去做工，完全是為了要作一個好弟弟。

　　小黑大三沒有做工了，他是資訊系的學生，大三都有做實驗的計劃，整個暑假都在電腦房裡，他自己說，他一定白了很多。

　　暑假快結束的時候，我看到小黑身旁多了一個年輕人，在他旁邊玩電腦，我覺得他有點面善，小黑替我介紹，原來這就是他弟弟，可是我怎麼樣都認不出來了。他過去不是個白面書生嗎？現在為什麼黑了好多，也強壯多了？

　　小黑的弟弟告訴我，他已經打了兩個暑假的苦工，都是在屏東，兩個暑假下來，他就永遠黑掉了，我忍不住問他，難道他也需要錢嗎？

　　小黑的弟弟笑了，黝黑的臉，露出了一嘴的白牙齒，他指著小黑對我說「我要當他的弟弟」。

　　在烈日下做了兩個暑假的苦工，他真的當成小黑的弟弟了。

◇ deceive (v.) 瞞；騙　　　　　　　　◇ familiar (adj.) 熟悉的

But I was not deceived. I knew that Darkie wasn't doing hard labor   **16-21**
just because he liked going shirtless and barefoot. If all he wanted
was that sort of enjoyment, all he had to do was go swimming. His
real reason for working, I knew, was to be a good brother.

Darkie didn't do any construction work the summer after his third
year. As an information engineering student, he had to spend his junior
year planning an experiment. He spent his whole summer vacation in
the computer lab. He said he was sure he had gotten a lot whiter.

When summer vacation was nearly over, I noticed a familiar-
looking young man playing on the computer next to Darkie. Darkie
introduced him to me: it was his younger brother! But why couldn't I
recognize him? Hadn't he been a white-faced bookworm? Why was
he so much darker and more muscular now?

Darkie's little brother told me that he had spent two summer
vacations doing construction work in Pingtung. Those two summers
had darkened him permanently. I couldn't help asking him, did he
also need the money that much?

Darkie's brother laughed, his dark face revealing a mouthful of white
teeth. Pointing at Darkie, he said to me, "I want to be his little bro."

After two summers of hard work under the blazing sun, he really
had become Darkie's little bro.

◇ permanently（adv.）永久地（與 temporarily 相對）

(1) by the sweat of one's brow 靠勞力 (2段)

His brother was a construction worker who earned his living by the sweat of his brow.

他哥哥就是一位完全靠勞力賺錢的建築工人。

解析

英文的 physical labor 指勞力，但在此為了讓文章增添趣味，所以使用出自於聖經中伊甸園的 by the sweat of one's brow 取代 physical labor。聖經上說，亞當在伊甸園從來都不必工作，某天他違反了上帝的旨意偷吃禁果，上帝責備他說：“In the sweat of thy face shalt thou eat thy bread, till though return unto the ground." (你必汗流滿面才得糊口，直到你歸了土。) 但因為我們大都是從眉際觀察到汗水，所以這個片語就演變為 by the sweat of one's brow。既然是勞動者必定會全身汗涔涔，但我們還是只以 brow 代替全體。畢竟 by the sweat of his hairy chest 聽起來並不是那麼文雅。

earn 這個字表示贏得或賺來，指的是需經一番努力才能獲得的。例如：可以說 Women earned the right to vote in the early twentieth century. 但當人們中獎時應該說 People win the lottery，之所以不說 earn the lottery，是因為中獎不是花費功夫才得到的。此外，當說某人 makes/earns a living 的時候，意思是說他只賺得僅供維持家計的薪水而已，這份薪水只能糊口並非發財，當然也就跟富有扯不上邊了。

小試身手

1-1. 漁夫越來越難賺到錢。

_____

1-2. 現在很少靠勞力維生的男人。

_____

(2) 文法概念：疑問代名詞開頭的名詞子句（3段）

What he told me gave me quite a shock.

他告訴我一件令我大吃一驚的事。

解析

如果我們把上面的英文原句依文法直譯成中文的話，就會變成「他所告訴我的(事)給了我相當的震驚」。注意在英文中並沒有明顯地指出所謂何「事」，而是藉由 what 一字來代替。疑問詞在英文裡除了當問句句首詢問他人之外，它還有很多其他用法。接下來我們來看看怎麼將 who, what, when, where, why, how 用在名詞子句裡。

◈ Who I am is not important.
　我是誰並不重要。

◈ He says he can't tell me where he works.
　他說他不可以告訴我他工作的地方。

◈ What to do about global warming is becoming a hot topic.
　如何面對全球化逐漸成為熱門話題了。

在上面的例句中，畫底線的部分都可視為是一個大名詞。有些名詞子句句首的疑問詞可以譯成中文，但有些卻不能，而有些卻要譯成與英文字面相異的字，例如：要把 what 譯成「如何」。用這三種情形來思考的話，就能清楚了解名詞子句的意思。下面的小試身手應該有助於闡述我的意思。

小試身手

2-1. 秋天是樹葉掉下的時候。

_____

2-2. 她究竟是如何逃走的，仍然是個謎。

_____

（3）文法概念：用介詞結束句子或子句（3段）

The clothing he had on when he was found clearly proved his identity.
他被發現時穿的衣服也有很清楚的記錄。

The clothes in the ad and the clothes Binghan had been found in matched perfectly.
那個廣告上的衣服和小黑當年被找到的完全吻合。

解析

英文老師通常都會要求學生不要用介系詞結束一個句子，但老實説這不是一個很好的規定，因為你會從以下的例子發現，英文有很多動詞片語以介系詞作結，例如：put on 穿上，turn off 關掉，hurry up 加快動作，joke around 開玩笑，find out 發現。

英文可以接受用動詞結束一個句子，當然也適用於動詞片語。既然動詞片語後面通常都是接介系詞，因此一些句子或句子中的子句就必然會以介系詞作結。原文第一個句子就是其中之一，had on clothing 意味著 be wearing it，而 the clothing he had on 正是「他當時穿的衣服」的唯一譯法。

然而有時候句子結尾的介系詞並非動詞片語的一部分。請見以下兩個例子：

◈ She wished she had someone to talk to.
她希望有人陪她説話。

◈ That's not the bed I usually sleep on.
那不是我平常睡的床。

雖然這些句子都可以改寫成把介系詞移向句中的句型，但整個句子卻會顯得奇怪又不乾脆：

◈ She wished she had someone with whom to talk.
◈ That's not the bed on which I usually sleep.

同樣地，原文第二個句子也可以改寫成：

◈ the clothes in which Binghan had been found

比起原文，這個改寫句較合乎文法規則，但是聽起來太過正式了，在日常口語中你幾乎不會聽到有人這麼説。

回到一開始所説的：為什麼有些英文老師不鼓勵學生把介系詞放在句尾呢？這是因為介系詞後通常都應該有受詞，例如：in the house，around the corner 等。然而，有時候受詞會比介系詞早一步出現在句子中。

例句一：talk to → someone
例句二：sleep on → the bed
故事引言：found in → the clothes

這樣看來，一個句子是可以用介系詞結尾的，只要它是動詞片語的一部分或是受詞已在句中出現即可。

如果你還是一頭霧水的話，重讀一次這則解説，然後接著做下面的練習，更能幫助理解。

小試身手

3-1. 那部電影什麼時候上映？

_____

3-2. 希望那件事可以讓你好好思考。

_____

3-3. 我不喜歡被騙。

_____

3-4. 我不懂他們是為了什麼事情而吵架。

_____

(4) straight shooter 說一是一的人；誠實而爽朗的人 (4段)

I told him he was a real straight shooter.

我告訴他小黑個性非常爽朗。

解析

有些人說話老愛拐彎抹角，他們很少表明心中所想，然而 straight shooter 就像子彈一樣非常直接。誠實爽朗的人通常都會是好朋友，因為你不必擔心他們是否會暗自心煩。這就是為什麼作者和社工決定馬上告訴小黑關於他身世的事：既然小黑對待他人都相當直率，直接告訴他事實應該也不會怎樣。

小試身手

4. 雖然不同意她大部分的看法，他還是佩服她的直率。

_____

(5) as long as I live 終生 (6段)

I'll call them Mom and Dad as long as I live.

我這一輩子都會認他們為爸爸媽媽。

解析

傳統結婚誓言都會以 till death do you part (直到死亡將你倆分開為止) 或是 as long as you both shall live (只要你倆一息尚存) 作為結尾。這個句型之所以特別的原因在於它常常用在承諾與誓言上，例如：

◇ After I nearly died of food poisoning, I swore never to eat another oyster as long as I lived.
在我差點死於食物中毒後，我發誓這輩子絕不再吃牡蠣。

5. 這是我的家，我這輩子都會待在這裡。

_____

（6）good samaritan 好心的人；願意幫忙的人（8段）

His parents were the classic rural good samaritan type.

他的爸爸媽媽是典型的鄉下好人。

解析

samaritan 一詞源自聖經，故事是一個猶太人到耶利哥旅遊，卻在當地遭遇竊賊襲擊，當他全身是傷、赤裸無助地被棄置在路旁時，兩個地位崇高的猶太人，一位祭司和一個利未人，從旁經過卻沒有停下來幫助他。後來一個撒瑪利亞人發現了他，憐憫之心油然而生，為他包紮傷口、給他衣服，並帶他到旅店，之後又拿錢給旅店老闆，請他照顧這個男人直到他恢復健康。

這個故事在聖經是相當有名的故事之一，其特別之處在於撒瑪利亞人與猶太人向來水火不容，但故事中的撒瑪利亞人卻還能同情受傷的猶太人。因此，只要有人能對他人抱持著異於常人的善心的話，英文就可以說他是 a good samaritan。

由於 samaritan 原本是指國籍，所以有時候第一個字母 s 會是大寫。

6. 當我們的車子拋錨時，剛好有個好心人經過，花了半天幫我們修好。

_____

（7）first thing in the morning 一大早就……（9段）

Then, first thing Saturday morning, we drove from Taichung to Taipei to "meet the parents."

星期六一早就從台中開車去台北「相親」。

解析

這個片語可以完全表示中文一大早的意思，即起床之後馬上做的事。如果到了半夜你已經太累而沒辦法完成作業的話，你或許會選擇先上床睡覺，等隔天早上醒了之後第一件事就是先完成它。它或許不會是你早上第一件做的事，畢竟你會先刷牙、吃早餐、沖澡，但之後你一定會馬上進行這件事。

小試身手

7. 有的人喜歡在下班以後去跑步，但是我喜歡一早就去。

_____

（8）strong 與 muscular 之間的差別（10段）

Although Darkie was a muscular kid, when he got out of the car he was a little weak at the knees.

小黑雖然是個壯漢，可是當他走下汽車的時候，兩腿都有點軟了。

解析

你或許已經發現有時候強壯被翻成 muscular，有時候卻翻成 strong。為什麼會有這樣的差異呢？在英文裡 strong 可以指很多種層面的強壯，例如：體力上、心理上、情感上等等。若是把上面句子裡的 muscular 換成 strong 的話，整句話的意思可能就會比較模糊，導致讀者可能會以為小黑是情感堅強而不是身體強壯。既然 muscular 只有身強體壯的意思的話，那整句的意思就會清楚許多。

然而，某些句子可以完全不用 muscular，因為整句話的語意指的就只有一種強壯。例如：

◈ He's as strong as an ox.
　 他強壯如牛。

另外，人們大多不會用 muscular 來形容自己，通常這個字都是拿來形容別人比較多。

小試身手

8-1. 我不夠強壯，抬不起這個石頭。

　　_____

8-2. 他樣子不像舉重選手，看起來不夠強壯。

　　_____

8-3. 要堅強──我知道妳一定可以度過這辛苦的時間。

　　_____

---

(9) much to someone's 情緒名詞／much to the 情緒名詞 of someone 令某人感到⋯⋯（10段）

He later told me that he had cried profusely on the train back to Taichung, much to the bewilderment of the people beside him.

事後，他告訴我，當天他在回台中的火車上，大哭一場，弄得旁邊的人莫名其妙。

解析

這是一個相當實用的片語，你可以把它放在句首或句尾表示令某人感到……。

例如：

◈ Much to my surprise, she remembered my birthday.
令我驚訝的是，她竟然記得我的生日。

◈ On the day of the picnic it rained, much to our dismay.
野餐那天下了雨，令我們很失望。

基本上就是把一個情緒名詞放在 much to someone's 的後面，用來表示個人或團體當時的情緒表現。而且這個片語一般都是以 much to someone's 情緒名詞來用，除非句子太長才會用 the 情緒名詞 of someone 來改寫，例如：原文中的 the people beside him 就太冗長了，把 bewilderment 加在後面會顯整個句子頭重腳輕且所有格用法也是個問題，因此才會改寫成 much to the bewilderment of the people beside him。

小試身手

9-1. 她講了半個小時的笑話，讓我們覺得很有趣。

_____

9-2. 他喝醉了站在桌子上開始脫衣服，弄得他的朋友都很不好意思。

_____

（10）have the 特質名詞 to 具備……的能力做……（10段）

Of course, my wife and I had the tact to only stay for half an hour.
我和太太當然識相地只坐了半小時就走了。

解析

tact 機靈是識相的必需特質。如果不夠靈敏的人可能會整天都待在小黑父母的家，完全不會察覺到這家人想要獨處的心情。但是作者和他的太太夠機靈，所以他們只待一會兒就先行離開了。

這個片語讓大家可以將長句子 Because someone had 某特質，he did...，簡化成 someone had the 特質 to do...。除了 tact 之外，decency 通情達理也可用在此句型，另外也還有其他用法。大家可以先從以下兩個例子開始記起：

◈ At least he had the decency to apologize.
　至少他氣量大，敢道歉。

◈ I don't have the brains to beat you in chess.
　我不夠聰明，下西洋棋下不過妳。

注意此句型在特質名詞後面的動詞一定是不定詞的形式。

小試身手

10-1. 她連等人家出電梯的禮貌都沒有，門一開，她就走進去。

_____

10-2. 他明智地避免在家庭聚會談政治。

_____

---

(11) take the liberty of 未經許可地；大膽地；冒昧（11段）

I had taken the liberty of telling Darkie's parents his size beforehand.
這也靠我事先通風報信，將小黑的尺寸告訴了他的親生父母。

解析

to take liberties 指的是隨意對待、隨便更改的意思。如你所知 liberty 意味著自由，想想紐約港的自由女神像(the Statue of Liberty)就知道了。在這個句型裡，它的意思是自由地做某件事，當沒人主動給予許可的時候，你就可以隨心所欲任意而為了。例如：

◈ Since no one seemed to be watching, I took the liberty of turning off the TV.
既然似乎沒人在看，我就擅自(未經許可地)關了電視機。

除了字面的意思之外，在文法上這個片語最重要的是後面的動詞一定是動名詞形式：

◈ I took the liberty of buying you some new clothes while you were gone.
當妳不在的時候，我擅自買了幾件新衣服給妳。

想必你現在已經注意到這個句型不一定只用在不好的事，通常是指需要冒險的事，或是一般人不會做的事。準備好放膽做了嗎？試試下面的例句吧。

小試身手

11-1. 她(未經我同意地)將我對公司的建議轉告老闆。

_____

11-2. 我告訴他不要那麼自作主張地用我的錢。

_____

11-3. 當我在外面讀大學的時候，我媽竟然讓客人睡我的房間。

_____

---

(12) go shirtless/barefoot 打赤膊／打赤腳(14段)

In fact, he said that whenever he worked, he went shirtless and barefoot, and it gave him more pleasure than anything.
他還告訴我他做工的時候，向來打赤膊打赤腳，這是他最痛快的時候。

解析

在英文中 go 就像中文的「打」，它是一個擁有許多不同意思的字，端看於上下文的語意而定。在這裡你可以把它當作是「以某種姿態到處走來走去」。或許你打籃球時喜歡打赤膊，又或許你在海灘時打赤腳。只要你夠大膽的話，你甚至可以全裸(go totally naked)如果沒其他人在你週遭的話。

注意像 shirtless, barefoot, naked 通常都是當形容詞用："shirtless construction worker", "barefoot doctor", "naked old man"。但是當你把 go 這樣的動詞放在前面的話，它們就會變成副詞，形容你是怎麼 go 的。有時候它們也可以當副詞與其他動詞連用："walk barefoot on the beach" "sit naked in the bathtub"。語言中的彈性能賦予你許多創造空間。

小試身手

12-1. 他可以赤腳踢足球而腳不會受傷。

_____

12-2. 在那邊打著赤膊、抽著菸的大漢就是領班。

_____

12-3. 如果你這麼厭倦洗衣服，何不赤裸幾天？

_____

小試身手解答

1-1. It's getting harder to make a living as a fisherman.

或 Fishermen are finding it more and more difficult to make a living.

1-2. Men who live by the sweat of their brow are rare nowadays.

2-1. Autumn is when the leaves fall.

2-2. How she escaped remains a mystery.

3-1. When does the movie come out?

3-2. Hopefully that will give you something to think about. (think about
→ something)

3-3. I don't like being lied to. (lie to → I)

3-4. I don't understand what they re fighting over/about. (fighting over
→ what)

4. Although he disagreed with most of her opinions, he admired her
for being a straight shooter.

5. This is my home—I m staying here as long as I live.

6. When our car broke down, a good samaritan who happened by
spent half the day helping us fix it.

7. Some people like to go running after work, but I like to go first
thing in the morning.

8-1. I'm not strong enough to lift this rock.

8-2. He doesn't look like a weightlifter—he's not muscular enough.

8-3. Be strong—I know you can make it through this tough time.

9-1. She told jokes for half an hour, much to our amusement.

9-2. He got drunk, stood on the table and started taking off his clothes, much to the embarrassment of his friends.

10-1. She doesn't even have the courtesy to wait for people to come out of the elevator—as soon as the door opens, she walks right in.

10-2. He has the wisdom to avoid political discussion at family gatherings.

11-1. She took the liberty of telling the boss my suggestions for the company.

11-2. I told him he needed to stop taking [so many] liberties with my money.

11-3. While I was away at college, my mom took the liberty of letting guests sleep in my room.

12-1. He can kick a football barefoot without hurting his foot.

12-2. The big shirtless guy over there smoking a cigarette is the foreman.

12-3. If you're so tired of doing laundry, why don't you just go naked for a few days?

The Bell Is Tolling Again
鐘聲又再響起

1-5　　我和阿傑都是暨南大學的學生，我們來到了這個學校以後，發現附近有好多好玩的地方可以去遊山玩水，一到週末，我和阿傑就到埔里附近去玩，第一年，我們只有腳踏車，第二年，我們都有了機車，出遊的範圍就越來越廣了。

　　有一天，我們來到了一個叫做倒影村的地方，忽然看到一個殘破的路標，路標指的地方是天籟村，現在是民國一百五十年(2061)，天籟村已經是被政府宣佈永遠歸還給大自然了。我們都知道，過去天籟村是有人住的，可是一次大地震震鬆了那裡的土質，以後每逢颱風或豪雨，就會有大規模的山崩和土石流災害，居民也就陸陸續續地搬離這個地方，3年前，最後一批居民離開了這個村，政府就宣佈天籟村不能再有人住了。政府切斷了水電，也在道路上設置了路障，從此天籟村就沒有人住了。

　　就因為那裡沒有人住，我和阿傑卻更想進去看看，道路雖然已經不能讓車子走，但是縣一八九號公路仍然可以步行，我們決定將機車停

CD2-2

◇ toll (v.) (鐘) 鳴響；敲
◇ freshman (n.) 大一生
◇ sophomore (n.) 大二生
◇ upgrade (v.) 升級
◇ broaden (v.) 使……更廣
◇ scope (n.) 範圍

◇ excursion (n.) 一日遊；短途旅行
◇ battered (adj.) 破破的
◇ point (v.) 指
◇ proclamation (n.) 宣言
◇ loosen (v.) 使……變鬆
◇ cloudburst (n.) 傾盆大雨

A-Jie and I are students at Chi Nan University. When we first came
to this school, we discovered there were all sorts of fun places in the
area with mountains and water that seemed made for our enjoyment.
As soon as the weekend arrived, A-Jie and I would head to the Puli
area for some fun. Freshman year we only had bicycles, but by
sophomore year we had upgraded to scooters, which broadened the
scope of our excursions considerably.

One day we had come to a place called Daoying Village when
we suddenly noticed a battered old road sign pointing toward
Tianlai Village. As of the current year of 2061, Tianlai Village has
been permanently returned to nature by government proclamation.
Everyone knows that there used to be people living in the village,
but a big earthquake loosened up the soil there, so that whenever
a typhoon or cloudburst came along after that, there were huge
landslides and mudslides. So the inhabitants gradually moved
away. When the last group departed three years ago, the government
declared that no one would be allowed to live in Tianlai again. They
cut the water and electricity and set up barricades in the road. The
village has been empty ever since.

The fact that no one lived there made A-Jie and me all the more
eager to see Tianlai for ourselves. The road had been rendered
impassable for vehicles, but County Highway 189 could be traversed

◇ landslide (n.) 土石滑動 (slids 是滑動
　的意思)
◇ inhabitant (n.) 居民
◇ declare (v.) 宣佈
◇ barricade (n.) 路障

◇ eager (adj.) 渴望的；興致勃勃的
◇ render (v.) 使……成為
◇ impassable (adj.) 不可通行的
◇ traverse (v.) 走過

在一個隱蔽的地方，沿著一八九號道路走進去。

　　這條道路兩旁大樹成蔭，一邊是山，一邊是一條小溪，偶爾可以看到一些被廢棄的房屋，這些房屋外面都長滿了綠色的爬籐，有些園子裡還可以看到當年人坐的椅子，有一次我們還看到了一輛生了銹的機車。

　　現在回想起來，我們不懂我們為什麼膽子這麼大，走了1個半小時，一個人也看不到，連一隻狗都沒有看到，倒是看到了各種的鳥，也看到了不少野兔，阿傑聲稱他驚鴻一瞥地看到一頭山豬。

6-10　　走了2個小時，我們終於到了天籟村，顯然，這裡曾經熱鬧過，我們看到派出所、衛生所、一些小店、一所小學、一些住家和一座教堂，我和阿傑這時才感到一點不安。看到這些倒坍的房屋，又看不到一個人影，總使我們兩個人想到一些科幻電影裡的情節。當然我們兩個都不願意講，我們強顏歡笑地四處看看，也拿了照相機照了一些相片。

　　在我們要打道回府的時候，忽然看到一間屋子裡居然有一位老先生

◈ shade (v.) 遮蔭
◈ abandon (v.) 遺棄
◈ creeper (n.) 匍匐植物
◈ vine (n.) 藤蔓植物

◈ rust (v.) 生鏽
◈ bold (adj.) 大膽的
◈ hare (n.) 野兔
◈ claim (v.) 聲稱

on foot. We decided to park our scooters out of sight and walk to the village along Highway 189.

The road was shaded by large trees growing along both sides. On one side were mountains; on the other was a stream. Occasionally we'd see a few abandoned houses, now overgrown with green creepers and vines. Some of the yards had chairs where people had used to sit, and once we even saw a rusted scooter.

Looking back on that day, we don't know what made us so bold as to walk for an hour and a half without seeing a single person or even a dog. We did see all kinds of birds, though, and quite a few hares. A-Jie claims he caught a glimpse of a mountain boar.

After two hours of walking, we finally arrived at Tianlai Village. That it had once been a bustling place was clear enough. We saw a police station, a health center, a few small stores, an elementary school, some homes and a chapel. Only now did A-Jie and I start to feel a little uneasy. Looking at these crumbling houses, without even a human shadow in sight, inevitably reminded us of certain sci-fi movies. Of course, we didn't want to say so out loud—instead, we forced ourselves to look cheerful while we looked around and took a few pictures.

6-10

Just as we were about to leave, we suddenly noticed an old man

---

◈ catch a glimpse of (n.) 瞥見（caught 為 catch 的不規則過去式）
◈ boar (n.) 野豬
◈ bustling (adj.) 熱鬧的

◈ crumble (v.) 粉碎
◈ inevitably (adv.) 難免地
◈ sci-fi (n/adj.) science fiction 的簡稱
◈ out loud (adv.) 出聲地

住在裡面，這位老伯伯衣服很整齊，頭髮梳得很好，鬍子也刮得很乾淨，他看到我們，極為高興，因為他已經好久沒有見到人了。

老先生是退休的電機工程師，他說他小的時候生長在這裡，國中一年級隨著父母到了台北，從此揮別了這個鄉下，在台北落地生根，他的學業很順利，進入電機系，做了一輩子有關電機的工作，家庭也很美滿。兩個兒子，一個兒子在美國，一個兒子在大陸，兩個人都全心全意地發展事業，無法常常和他見面，他的老伴在2年前去世，大約一個月以前，他忽發奇想，找人將這裡的舊房子整修了一下，又回到這裡來住了。

老先生帶我們四處去張望，他顯然對這裡的一草一木，都嚮往不已，他告訴我，他永遠也忘不了那所小學，這所小學雖然有些改變，但改變得不大，現在當然是雜草叢生，但是房舍仍在。大多數的小學校舍都很制式化，但這座校舍卻很雅，牆壁是磨石子的，每根柱子都嵌入紅色的石子，一望就想起原住民的藝術。老伯伯告訴我們這是大地震以後的建築，特別美。

◇ immaculate (adj.) 非常乾淨的
◇ neatly (adv.) 整齊地
◇ retire (v.) 退休
◇ bid (v.) （正式）向……表示（bade 為 bid 的不規則過去式）
◇ settle down (v.) 安定下來
◇ spend (v.) 度過
◇ devote to (v.) 奉獻於
◇ on impulse (adv.) 出於衝動地
◇ irresistible (adj.) 無法抵擋的

living in one of the houses! His clothes were immaculate, his hair neatly combed, his face clean-shaven. When he saw us, he became very excited, for we were the first people he had seen in a long, long time.

The old gentleman, a retired electrical engineer, said that Tianlai had been his home as a child. During his first year of middle school, he followed his parents to Taipei and bade his rural home farewell. He settled down in Taipei and did very well in school, being accepted to an electrical engineering department and spending his entire career working in that field. He had a happy family, too. Two sons, one in America and one in China, both highly devoted to their work and thus unable to see him very often. His wife had passed away two years before. About a month ago, totally on impulse, he got someone to fix up his old house and came back here to live.

The old gentleman gave us a brief tour. It was obvious that every vine and tree held an irresistible attraction for him. He would never forget his old elementary school, he told me—although it had changed somewhat, it was mostly the same. It was now overgrown with weeds, of course, but the building was still there. The great majority of elementary school buildings are built in the same standardized fashion, but this one was elegant, with smooth stone walls and red pebbles inlaid in each pillar, after the manner of aboriginal art. It

◈ attraction (n.) 吸引力；魅力
◈ standardized (adj.) 標準化的
◈ fashion (n.) 樣式
◈ elegant (adj.) 雅緻的
◈ smooth (adj.) 平滑的

◈ pebble (n.) 小石子
◈ inlaid (adj.) 嵌入的
◈ pillar (n.) 柱子
◈ manner (n.) 方法

我們走到了那座教堂,教堂是紅磚造的,教堂外面有一個很高的架子,架子上有一座鐘,我和阿傑大喜過望,搶著去搖動繩子來敲鐘,鐘聲清脆無比,而且好像可以傳得好遠,這種在山谷中打鐘的動作,僅僅在夢裡夢到過,我和阿傑都為了能夠敲鐘而興奮不已。

11-15　　老伯伯告訴我們,這座鐘過去是不能亂打的,因為當年,這座鐘是用來傳遞信息的,有人生孩子,鐘敲10下,有人去世,鐘敲12下,有人生重病,快去世了,鐘敲17下,意思是大家應該為他的靈魂祈禱。鐘敲8下,大概是叫大家來開會,鐘敲11下,是叫大家來望彌撒,至於每天黃昏的時候,鐘聲是要大家靜下心來晚禱。

老伯伯小時候對鐘聲沒有甚麼感覺,只覺得好玩,他記得有一次晚上鐘聲響了,他的媽媽聽了鐘聲以後,就走到村子裡一戶人家去,因為她知道有一位老太太要去世了。她必須去安慰老太太的家人……

◇ elated (adj.) 高興極了　　　　◇ thrill (n.) 刺激
◇ crisp (adj.) 清脆的　　　　　　◇ urge (v.) 勸

had been built after the earthquake, the old man told us, so it was especially beautiful.

We walked over to the red brick chapel, outside of which was a high tower from which a bell hung. A-Jie and I were elated. We rushed over and pulled on the rope to ring the bell. Its sound was incredibly pure and crisp, and it seemed to travel very far. Ringing a bell like this in a mountain valley was something we had only dreamed of—it was quite a thrill for A-Jie and me to do it in real life.

The old man told us that in the old days, you couldn't just ring the bell whenever you wanted to because it was used to send messages. When a child was born, the bell tolled ten times; when someone died, it tolled 12 times; when someone was sick and about to die, it tolled 17 times to urge the villagers to pray for his soul. If the bell tolled 8 times, it was usually to call a town meeting; by tolling 11 times, it summoned the villagers for Mass. And every day at dusk, the sound of the bell would remind the people to put aside their worldly cares for evening prayer.

11-15

As a child, the old man had no special feelings about the bell—he just thought it was fun. He remembered one evening when his mother walked to a neighbor's house after hearing the bell ring because she knew that an old woman there was about to pass away and she had to go to comfort the family....

◇ summon (v.) 召集
◇ dusk (n.) 黃昏

◇ put aside (v.) 擱在一旁
◇ care (n.) 煩惱

　　可是他離開這個村子以後，卻又懷念這個鐘聲了，因為鐘聲代表人與人之間的相互關懷。

　　在這個村子裡，誰都認識誰，所謂雞犬相聞也。村民們相互分享大家的喜樂，也分擔大家的憂傷。他在台北，住在一個公寓，隔壁住的是誰，他常常弄不清楚。鄰居搬走了，他也不知道。這麼多年來，他一直懷念著這個鐘聲，因為鐘聲代表一個互相關懷的社會。他說他曾經感覺過互相關懷的滋味，老了以後，越發懷念這種感覺。

　　我和阿傑不約而同地告訴老伯伯，我們知道如何進來，我們以後有空，一定會再來看看他的，老伯伯卻說他可能在短期內要離開了。太陽快下山，老伯伯催我們離開。他說我們必須在天黑之前走回倒影村，他說萬一迷路，就沿著河往低處走，一定會走回文明的。我們只好走了。走了約10分鐘以後，忽然鐘聲又再響起，這次我們數了一下，鐘聲一共是17下，我們都記得，這表示有人病重，已經快去世了。阿傑說，怪不得老伯伯說他快離開了，所謂落葉歸根也。

◇ miss (v.) 想念
◇ symbolize (v.) 象徵；代表
◇ care (n.) 關心 (注意這裡的用法和上面的「煩惱」不一樣)
◇ concern (n.) 掛念

◇ bear (v.) 承擔 (borne 為不規則過去式)
◇ warmth (n.) 溫暖
◇ mutual (adj.) 互相的
◇ strike (v.) 心念一動
◇ press (v.) 催促

After leaving the village, however, he missed the sound of the bell, for its tolling symbolized the care and concern people have for one another.

In the village, everybody knew everybody—even their dogs and chickens could hear each other. The villagers had shared one another's joys and borne one another's sorrows. In Taipei, the old man had lived in an apartment, where he often didn't know the people next door—a neighbor might move away without him even noticing. For all these years, he had been missing the tolling of the bell because the bell symbolized a society where people cared for one another. Having once felt the warmth of mutual concern, he said he missed it even more in his old age.

Both struck with the same thought, A-Jie and I told the old gentleman that since we now knew the way to the village, we would come back and see him sometime. But he said he would probably be leaving in the near future. The sun was setting; the old man pressed us to be on our way. He said we should be sure to get back to Daoying Village before nightfall. If we got lost, all we had to do was follow the river downhill and we would make it back to civilization for sure. And so we reluctantly set off. After walking for about 10 minutes, suddenly we heard the bell toll again. We counted the number of times 17. This, we remembered, meant that someone was ill and close to death. No wonder the old man had said he would be leaving soon, observed A-Jie—as the poet said, the fallen leaf returns to its roots.

◇ reluctantly (adv.) 不捨地　　　　◇ observe (v.) 說道

16-17　　我們兩個人，大概一輩子都不會忘記那代表著互相關懷的鐘聲。前些日子，有一位同學出了車禍，我們一起去醫院看他，有好一陣子，他都在昏迷之中，我們平時嘻嘻哈哈的同學們，現在都很擔心地等著他醒過來。阿傑和我都在場，他悄悄地問我一句話：「老李，你有沒有聽到鐘聲又響起了。」我告訴他，我也聽到了。事實上，我們都發現，只要我們關懷別人，天籟村的鐘聲就會響起。

　　我們曾經又去倒影村一次，但我們找不到天籟村的入口了，雖然天籟村永遠消失了，但我和阿傑卻一直常常聽到那裡的鐘聲，因為我們知道天籟村鐘聲深刻而特殊的意義。

◇ ideal (n.) 理想
◇ coma (n.) 昏迷的狀態
◇ joke around (v.) 開玩笑；胡鬧
◇ anxiously (adv.) 著急地

I don't think the two of us will ever forget that bell and the ideals **16-17** it represented. A few days ago, one of our classmates was in an accident, and a group of us went to the hospital to visit him. He's been in a coma for some time now. Instead of laughing and joking around like usual, we now wait anxiously for him to awaken. In the hospital, A-Jie asked me, "Old Lee, do you hear the bell tolling again?" I told him I heard it too. In fact, both of us have discovered that as long as we care about others, the bell in Tianlai Village will continue to toll.

Once we went back to Daoying Village, but we couldn't find the entrance to Tianlai. Although Tianlai Village is gone forever, A-Jie and I often hear the tolling of the bell there, for we understand its profound and unique significance.

◈ profound (adj.) 深刻的　　　　　　◈ significance (n.) 意涵

(1) when 作為連接詞(2段)

One day we had come to a place called Daoying Village when we suddenly noticed a battered old road sign pointing toward Tianlai Village.

有一天，我們來到了一個叫做倒影村的地方，忽然看到一個殘破的路標，路標指的地方是天籟村。

解析

如同我在序言裡所說的一樣，中文對於連接詞和標點符號不會太過要求。只要把逗點放在中文原句的「地方」和「路標」之後，就能把整句話斷成三個獨立的句子。而把這些句子翻成英文就會變成

1. One day we came to a place called Daoying Village.
2. Suddenly we saw a battered old road sign.
3. The sign pointed toward Tianlai Village.

接下來我們只要把這些字句連結成具有邏輯性的句子就行了。為了符合英文文法的要求，我們要做的比只加逗點的中文還多。要串起第二和第三個句子相當簡單，既然兩句裡都有 sign 這個字，我們就可以把第三句改成形容子句來形容第二句裡的路標：

◈ Suddenly we saw a battered old road sign pointing toward Tianlai Village.

或者也可以改寫成如下，

◈ Suddenly we saw a battered old road sign that pointed toward Tianlai Village.

接著要把第一句也加上來，這時可以想像就在來到倒影村後突然看到路標。為了要突顯第一個動作的完成性，我們得用完成式改寫一下動詞形態。

◈ One day we had come to a place called Daoying Village...

我們可以使用連接詞 when 說明接下來發生了什麼事，

◇ One day we had come to a place called Daoying Village when suddenly we saw a battered old road sign pointing toward Tianlai Village.

這樣就大功告成了！這個句子文法正確，但如果能把 suddenly 和 we 的順序對調，且用 noticed 替換 saw 的話，會更順暢。

我發現像這樣的斷句能讓翻譯事半功倍，下次如果你要翻譯一個長句子，特別是將外語翻譯成母語時，可以試著把句子分開成簡單易懂的字句，再一一翻譯它們。當你這麼做的時候，你也差不多要完成翻譯的工作了，因為剩下來要做的就只是用合乎邏輯的方式把這些小句子流暢地連結起來而已。你不必一開始就把每個句子翻得盡善盡美，只要清楚地表達句子的意思即可。

小試身手

1. 我剛下班回家，正在看電視，就聽到了這個消息。

_____

---

(2) 由形容詞來的動詞：broaden（使……更廣）；loosen（使……更鬆）（1段、2段）

Freshman year we only had bicycles, but by sophomore year we had upgraded to scooters, which broadened the scope of our excursions considerably.

第一年，我們只有腳踏車，第二年，我們都有了機車，出遊的範圍就越來越廣了。

Everyone knows that there used to be people living in the village, but a big earthquake loosened up the soil there.

我們都知道，過去天籟村是有人住的，可是一次大地震震鬆了那裡的土質。

解析

將英文中的形容詞變成動詞最普遍方法或許是在字尾加上-en。例如：

soften	使……更軟	shorten	使……更短
harden	使……更硬	tighten	使……更緊
thicken	使……更厚／更濃	gladden	使……快樂
fatten	使……更胖	sadden	使……難過

下面也有兩個動詞在詞幹上有著不規則變化

| embolden | 使……更大膽 |
| lengthen | 使……更長 |

當你看到一個字以 -en 結尾，而且你不清楚它的意思時，可以看看它是不是從你熟悉的字演變而來的。但是要記住並非所有的形容詞都可以用這樣的方式變成動詞，就像英文並沒有 thinnen, slowen, happyen 這樣的字。

另外值得注意的是 upgrade 這個字。它常用在現在的 E 世代，當舊裝置或軟體被淘汰，轉向更新更好的科技時就會用到這個字（可當動詞或名詞）。最後，scope 這個字通常用在抽象的事物上，像是計畫（plan）、調查（investigation）等，而且也不同於 scale，即使這兩者常常都被翻成「規模」或「範圍」。

小試身手

2-1. 他們準備要拓寬這條路。

_____

2-2. 完整討論英文文法會超出這本書的範圍。

_____

2-3. 聽說她終於升級用數位相機了。

_____

(3) the fact that... ⋯⋯的事實；⋯⋯這件事情(3段)

The fact that no one lived there made A-Jie and me all the more eager to see Tianlai for ourselves.

就因為那裡沒有人住，我和阿傑卻更想進去看看(天籟村)。

解析

大部分的美語母語人士很常使用這三個字。當你想要將一個事實、片語或想法放進一個句子時，最快的方式就是把它當成名詞來看。但是 no one lived there 是一個完整句子，並非名詞或名詞片語，這時我們要怎麼把它當作 made 的主詞呢？只要在它前面加上 the fact that 就行了，它的意思就是「正是沒有人住那裡這件事情讓我和阿傑很想進去看看」。

要解說在何時和怎麼使用這三個字不太容易，但學會使用這個片語將有助於大大提昇你的英文能力。以下有幾個例子供大家參考：

◈ The fact that none of our representatives in Russia speaks Russian is cause for concern.
我們在俄羅斯的代表沒有一個人會說俄文這件事讓人憂心。

◈ What upsets me is the fact that she made the decision without consulting anyone.
讓我心煩的是她沒詢問任何人就做了這個決定。

◈ In today's atmosphere of economic pessimism, it is easy to forget the fact that most of us are still better off than our parents were at our age.
現今的經濟悲觀氣氛讓人容易忘記我們大部分的人仍然過得比我們父母當年還要好。

另外也有長句子，但只要你知道它們是怎麼存在於句子之後，就不需要害怕了。

小試身手

3-1. 他發現他很難接受自己已經五十歲的事實。

_____

3-2. 他是同性戀的事實跟他藝術作品的品質沒有關係。

_____

（4）instead（6段、16段）

Of course, we didn't want to say so out loud—instead, we forced ourselves to look cheerful while we looked around and took a few pictures.

當然我們兩個都不願意講，我們強顏歡笑地四處看看，也拿了照相機照了一些相片。

Instead of laughing and joking around like usual, we now wait anxiously for him to awaken.

我們平時嘻嘻哈哈的同學們，現在都很擔心地等著他醒過來。

解析

Instead 應該是所有的英文字中，我最希望有相對應中文翻譯的字了。我想大部分的台灣人都是在學校學到這個字，但我卻很少聽到他們在說英文時用到這個字。要瞭解這個字，如果先知道 stead 的意思會更有幫助，stead 以前常用來指地方或是位置，特別是已經被別人佔用的位置。就算到了現在，你也會看到類似這樣的句子 "she went to the meeting in my stead"（她代替我與會）。

第一個原文例句中，阿傑和作者本來可以對空曠詭異的天籟村表現出恐懼的神情，但他們卻決定要強顏歡笑。也就是說相對於恐懼，他們選擇了另一種作法。同樣地，第二個原文例句，同學們對車禍朋友的關心讓他們的舉止異於平常的嘻笑怒罵。由於 instead 這個字沒有相對應的中文翻譯，所以當你翻譯類似句子的時候，它也就不會是你第一個想到的字了。

當你讀或聽英文的時候，請留意 instead 的用法，如此一來你就能很快的瞭解竅門所在。要注意它是怎麼出現在句子前後的，並試著理解何時後面要加 of。大家可以從以下的練習開始學起。

小試身手

4-1. 我們本來要看電影，結果(決定)提早睡覺。

_____

4-2. 與其徒然抱怨，何不試著改善這個情況？

_____

---

(5) overgrown with 長滿了 (雜草等) (4段、9段)

Occasionally we'd see a few abandoned houses, now overgrown with green creepers and vines.
偶爾可以看到一些被廢棄的房屋，這些房屋外面都長滿了綠色的爬籐。

It was now overgrown with weeds, of course, but the building was still there.
現在當然是雜草叢生，但是房舍仍在。

解析

把 overgrown 拆開來看應該很容易就能猜到它的意思。不過特別的是這個字一定都是過去分詞形式，且後面接著介系詞 with 指出是什麼植物叢生。

grown 絕對不是唯一能用 over 加在字首的字。以下是其他的例子：

overdo	做過頭
overestimate	高估
overstate	説過頭

中文也有相對應的説法，如「她做得太 over」。

當然，其他動詞也能把 under 加在字尾，而有些字的意思剛好與 over-相反，

understand	了解
underthrow	(打球)傳／投得不夠遠
undervalue	(資產)把價值估得太低

下面的練習中，我各以大家可能不熟悉的 under- 和 over- 動詞造句，請利用這些動詞把句子翻成英文吧。

小試身手

5-1. 我再怎麼強調這方案對我們公司的重要性都不為過。(overemphasize)

_____

5-2. 從歷史上來看，窮人通常被他們的政府忽視。(underserve)

_____

5-3. 她的工作是監管當地的教育體系。(oversee)

_____

(6) strike 的諸多用法(15段)

Both struck with the same thought, A-Jie and I told the old gentleman that since we now knew the way to the village, we would come back and see him sometime.

我和阿傑不約而同地告訴老伯伯，我們知道如何進來，我們以後有空，一定會再來看看他的。

解析

棒球迷都知道好球的英文是 strike，但通常它是用來指打擊。如同單字解說所示，being struck with a thought 就像是中文的心念一動，在這裡屬於比較抽象的說法，說明一個人彷彿突然被一個想法襲擊一般。strike 的三種說法都值得一學。

小試身手

6-1. 據說閃電不會兩次都打到同一個地方。

_____

6-2. 三個好球你就出局了。

_____

6-3. 突然間他想到一個報紙社論的主題。

_____

---

(7) get back to; make it back to 回到(15段)

He said we should be sure to get back to Daoying Village before nightfall. If we got lost, all we had to do was follow the river downhill and we would make it back to civilization for sure.

他說我們必須在天黑之前走回倒影村，他說萬一迷路，就沿著河往低處走，一定會走回文明的。

解析

這些片語以及 be back 都常用來取代 return 這個動詞。例如，當一個女生去她朋友家，她父母可能會問，

◈ What time will you be back?
妳幾點要回來？

make it back 通常隱含人比預定回來的時間晚很多，很有可能是因為他們在途中遭遇困難。例如：

◈ It was ten o'clock at night when I finally made it home from work.
當我終於得以從工作抽身回到家時，已經是晚上十點了。

小試身手

7-1. 瑪莉姑姑昨天晚上剛從歐洲回來

_____

7-2. 那天晚上有十個軍人出去巡邏，卻只有九個回到了基地。

_____

小試身手解答

1. I had just arrived home from work and was watching TV when I heard the news.

2-1. They are getting ready to widen this road.

2-2. A full discussion of English grammar would be beyond the scope of this book.

2-3. I hear she finally upgraded to a digital camera.

3-1. He's finding it hard to accept the fact that he has turned 50.

3-2. The fact that he is gay has nothing to do with the quality of his art.

4-1. We had planned to see a movie, but we ended up going to bed early instead.

4-2. Instead of just complaining, why don't you try to improve the situation?

5-1. I cannot overemphasize this project's importance for our company.

5-2. Historically, poor people have been underserved by their governments.

5-3. Her job is to oversee the local school system.

6-1. They say that lightning never strikes the same place twice.

6-2. Three strikes and you're out.

6-3. Suddenly he was struck with an idea for a newspaper editorial.

7-1. Aunt Mary just got back from Europe last night.

7-2. Ten soldiers went out on patrol that night, but only nine made it back to base.

The Grass-Covered Graveyard

那青草覆地的墓園

1-5　　　我的爸爸就葬在附近，所以我可以常常去掃墓，去墓園有時會四處逛逛，我發現在公墓的邊緣有一片草地，草地上有一棵大樹，每年春天，這棵大樹會開白色的花，花瓣落在草地，非常好看。我一開始以為這裡僅僅是草地而已，可是我後來發現有人常常在草地上撒一些花，我開始懷疑草地下也許有人葬著。

　　　果真，公墓管理員告訴我，這裡的確葬了人。有些流浪漢去世以後，政府就將他們葬在這裡，也有些窮人死了以後，沒有任何錢辦葬禮，政府也會幫他們買一口極便宜的棺木，葬在這裡。最近，流浪漢也好，窮人也好，都經過火化，骨灰也是埋在這裡。

　　　過去，這裡簡直沒有人管，後來開始有些善心人士來將環境整理一下，有一位無名氏捐了一大筆錢，將這裡鋪上草地，種了這棵樹，而且每年寄錢來，要求政府將這片草地維持得很好。

　　　我慢慢地發現有一位中年人，大概四十歲左右，常來替草地整理環

CD2-4
◇ bury（v.）埋葬
◇ tidy up（v.）整理
◇ grave（n.）墳墓
◇ stroll（v.）溜達
◇ cemetery（n.）墓園
◇ edge（n.）邊緣
◇ grounds（n.）（屬於教會、學校等的）園地
◇ petal（n.）花瓣
◇ scatter（v.）撒
◇ wonder（v.）好奇
◇ inform（v.）告知

My father is buried near here, so I often go and tidy up his grave.
Sometimes when I visit I stroll around the cemetery, which is how
I discovered the grassy field at the edge of the grounds. A big
tree is planted in the field, and every spring, when it blooms with
white blossoms, the petals fall onto the grass, and the field is lovely
indeed. At first I thought it was nothing more than a field, but later I
discovered that someone often came to scatter flowers over the grass.
That made me wonder whether anyone was buried underneath.

Sure enough, the man in charge of the graveyard informed me that
there were people buried there. When a drifter died, the government
would often bury him under the field. Likewise, when a poor man
died without enough money to pay for a funeral, the government
would buy him a cheap coffin and inter him there. These days,
drifters and poor people alike are cremated, and their ashes are buried
in the field.

The field was once neglected, but eventually a few good-hearted
people cleaned it up, and an anonymous donor gave a large sum to
plant the grass and the tree. The donor sent money to the government
each year to keep the field looking nice.

After a while I noticed a middle-aged man—probably about forty—

◇ drifter (n.) 流浪漢（漂流者）
◇ likewise (adv.) 同樣地
◇ funeral (n.) 喪禮
◇ coffin (n.) 棺材
◇ inter (v.) 〔比較正式〕埋葬
◇ cremate (v.) 火葬

◇ neglect (v.) 忽視；不管
◇ eventually (adv.) 到後來；到最後
◇ anonymous (adj.) 匿名的
◇ donor (n.) 捐者
◇ sum (n.) 筆〔錢〕

境，我發現他好像很和善，就跑去和他搭訕。他說他的爸媽在年輕的時候，有一天去殯儀館參加一個葬禮，發現隔壁有一個非常簡陋的葬禮，一位道士在五分鐘內唸完了經文，一位年輕的女子在旁邊哭泣，他們才知道女子的年輕丈夫死了，她丈夫的病用盡了所有的積蓄，現在她連棺材都買不起，還好政府出錢幫她買了一口最便宜的薄皮棺材，中年人爸媽好奇心起，跟著年輕的寡婦到達了公墓，發現這位窮苦的年輕人沒有能葬入公墓，只能葬在公墓外圍的地方，當然也沒有立石碑。中年人的爸媽以後常常來做整理環境的義工，他們也鼓勵他來，現在他的爸媽都已過世，他這個習慣都已養成了。

清明節到了，公墓裡擠滿了來掃墓的人，我去那片草地上看看，忽然發現了那位中年人，這次我認出了他。昨天晚上，我在一個新聞節目中，看到一位記者介紹一個台灣富有家族的墓園，這個墓園背山面海，氣派非凡，記者說所有的風水師都說這個墓園風水好，難怪他們

◈ maintain (v.) 維持
◈ mortuary (n.) 殯儀館
◈ budget (n.) 預算
◈ memorial (adj.) 紀念的
◈ service (n.) 儀式

◈ go on (v.) 進行
◈ sacred (adj.) 神聖的
◈ weep (v.) 哭泣(wept 為 weep 的不規則過去式)
◈ deceased (n.) 往生者

who frequently came to maintain the field. He seemed friendly enough, so I walked over to him and said hello. He told me that his parents, when they were young, were attending a funeral at a mortuary when they discovered an extremely low-budget memorial service going on in the room next to them. A Taoist priest read a sacred text for no more than five minutes while a young woman wept beside him. They found out that the deceased was her husband; she had spent all their savings trying to cure his illness, and now she couldn't even afford a coffin for him. At least the government had paid for a thin wooden coffin of the cheapest variety. Their curiosity aroused, the forty-year-old man's parents followed the young widow to the cemetery, where they discovered that the poor woman's husband was not buried in an actual grave, but on the edge of the grounds, without a headstone of course. After that, the forty-year-old man's parents regularly took time to clean up the area as volunteers, and they encouraged him to come as well. Now both his parents had passed away, but not before instilling the same habit in him.

On Tomb Sweeping Day, the cemetery was crowded with people tidying up their family members' graves. I headed over to the field to have a look, where to my surprise I found the forty-year-old man. This time I recognized him. While watching the news the night before, I saw a reporter report on the private graveyard of a rich Taiwanese family. Backed by mountains and facing the sea, the

◇ afford (v.) 買得起
◇ arouse (v.) 激起
◇ widow (n.) 寡婦

◇ headstone (n.) 墓石
◇ instill (v.) (藉著榜樣或教導而)灌輸

如此有錢，記者也訪問了這個家族中的一個成員。當時我就覺得有些面善，原來就是這位經常來做善事的義工。

6-10　這次他帶了太太和兩個兒子，兩個兒子都在草地上撒下一枝一枝的黃菊花，青青草地上現在到處都是黃菊花，我覺得這似乎有點不尋常。

中年人看到了我，微笑地和我打招呼。我問他是不是就是那一位富有家庭的成員，他說是的。我又問他是不是來掃墓的？他點點頭，然後告訴我一個驚人的事情，他說他的爸爸媽媽就葬在這裡，這片草地之下。

他的媽媽活著的時候，一直默默地照顧好多的窮人，是她寄錢給公墓，將這片亂葬之地變成了青草覆地的墓園。她說服了中年人的爸爸，他爸爸死了之後，大斂儀式之中，有短短的一段時間，只有他這個獨子和一位老傭人陪著棺木，他們將爸爸的遺體從昂貴的棺木中搬了出來，放進了薄皮棺材，昂貴棺木蓋上，裡面已經是空的，卻沒有人知道，晚上老傭人負責將他爸爸葬到這裡來。後來媽媽也去世了，

◇ impressive（adj.）令人印象深刻；令人敬佩
◇ geomancer（n.）風水師
◇ feng shui（n.）風水
◇ none other than（ph.）不是別人就是
◇ chrysanthemum（n.）菊花
◇ practically（adv.）幾乎；簡直
◇ shocking（adj.）驚人的
◇ multitude（n.）一大群
◇ plot（n.）塊（土地）

graveyard was impressive. According to the reporter, the geomancers all agreed it had good feng shui—small wonder the family was so rich. The reporter interviewed one of the members of the family. I knew he looked familiar—it turned out he was none other than the volunteer who often came to do good.

This time he had his wife and two sons with him. The boys were scattering yellow chrysanthemums on the ground; they had practically covered the whole field with flowers. This seemed a little out of the ordinary, I thought.

6-10

When the man saw me, he smiled and said hello. I asked him if he really was a member of the rich family; he said he was. Then I asked him whether he had come to tidy up his family members' graves. He nodded, then told me a shocking truth: his mother and father were buried right there, under the grass.

When his mother was alive, she had always quietly cared for a multitude of poor people. It was she who had sent money to the cemetery to turn this plot of makeshift burial sites into a grass-covered graveyard. She had also persuaded his father to go along with her idea: when the father died, there was a brief time during the burial ceremony when only his son and an old servant were beside the coffin. Together, they removed the body from its luxurious casket and placed it in a thin wooden coffin. Then they replaced the lid on the

◈ makeshift (adj.) 臨時的
◈ persuade (v.) 說服
◈ go along with (v.) 依從
◈ ceremony (n.) 典禮

◈ luxurious (adj.) 奢華的
◈ casket (n.) 棺材（和coffin 一樣）
◈ lid (n.) 蓋子

又被偷偷地葬到了這裡。

　　媽媽叮囑兒子，不要知道爸爸媽媽確切的下葬地方，只要知道他們是葬在這片青草之下就可以了。所以他每次在青草地上撒花，都要到處撒下去，他知道他的爸爸媽媽希望他不僅想到爸爸媽媽，也想到那些幾乎死無葬身之地的窮人。

　　我看到了世界上最美的墓園。而且我有一個奇特的想法，每次看到青青的草原，我就會想到我的祖先，他們一定也是葬在草地之下，不然葬在哪裡呢？

◈ furtively (adv.) 偷偷地
◈ fashion (n.) 方式
◈ admonish (v.) 勸

◈ take note of (v.) 留意
◈ lie (v.) 躺(lay 為 lie 的不規則過去式)
◈ nearly (adv.) 幾乎；差一點

expensive casket: it was now empty, but no one knew. That night, the old servant buried the man's father under the field. Later, his mother died too and was furtively laid to rest in like fashion.

The mother admonished her son not to take note of the exact place where she and her husband were buried—all he needed to know was that they lay somewhere under the field. Thus, every time he scattered flowers over the grass, he scattered them everywhere, for he knew that his parents wished him to think not only of them, but of all the people so poor that they nearly died without a place to be buried.

I saw the world's most beautiful graveyard. And now I have a strange tendency to think of my ancestors whenever I see a grassy field. They are undoubtedly buried there—where would they be otherwise?

◈ tendency (n.) 傾向
◈ ancestor (n.) 祖先

◈ otherwise (adv.) 不然

（1） nothing more than ……而已；只不過是……（1 段）

At first I thought it was nothing more than a field, but later I discovered that someone often came to scatter flowers over the grass.

我一開始以為這裡僅僅是草地而已，可是我後來發現有人常常在草地上撒一些花。

解析

希望你已經熟悉 "more than" （多於）與 "less than" （少於）的用法。例：

◈ Less than half of you passed the test.
考試及格的人數不到你們的一半。

◈ I always want more than what I have.
我想要的總比我擁有的多。

小試身手

1-1. 她自稱為記者，實際上只不過是個騙子。

_____

1-2. 這是個不折不扣的災難。

_____

（2） whether; if 是不是（1 段、7 段）

That made me wonder whether anyone was buried underneath.
(那件事情使)我開始懷疑草地下也許有人葬著。

I asked him if he really was a member of the rich family; he said he was.
我問他是不是就是那一位富有家庭的成員，他說是的。

Then I asked him whether he had come to tidy up his family members' graves.

我又問他是不是來掃墓的？

解析

許多美國人在說中文時都會犯下列錯誤。舉例來說，他們不說「不知道你願不願意」（"I don't know if you'd be willing to..."），反而模仿英文裡的說法說成「不知道如果願意」。然而我從未聽過一個台灣人犯同樣的錯誤，因為要去理解 "I don't know if you're willing not willing" 並不難，姑且不論它是否合乎英文文法。首先你必須用 "if"或是 "whether" 取代「是不是」、「有沒有」、「喜不喜歡」等詞。舉例來說，你要問，「我問過她會不會游泳」。我們必須將動詞轉換成過去式：

I asked her if she could swim. （NOT "can"）或是

I asked her if she knew how to swim. （NOT "knows how to"）

注意到基本上不論你是用 "if" 或 "whether" 都沒什麼不同。下個例子中我們將使用 "whether" 來替代。舉例來說，「我好奇她有沒有去過台南」。套用第一個步驟你將得出：

I wonder whether...

因為我們現在是用「現在式」在說話，沒有轉換時態的必要。

I wonder whether she has ever been to Tainan.

在這個例子中，"if" 和 "whether" 都扮演著連接詞的角色，串接著兩個分別的子句。通常第一個子句會用 "ask" 或是 "wonder" 這一類動詞，而第二個子句表示你所問或是所想之事。

小試身手

2-1. 他問我要不要陪他去看電影。

_____

2-2. 不知道〔我好奇〕這個週末會不會下雨。

_____

3. would 會（will）的過去式（2 段）

When a drifter died, the government would often bury him under the field. Likewise, when a poor man died without enough money to pay for a funeral, the government would buy him a cheap coffin and inter him there.

有些流浪漢去世以後，政府就將他們葬在這裡，也有些窮人死了以後，沒有任何錢辦葬禮，政府也會幫他們買一口極便宜的棺木，葬在這裡。

解析

此為 "If/when X, then Y will happen"（如果 X，Y 就會發生。）的過去式同義詞。將句子的關鍵釐清會清楚得出：

◇ when a drifter died → the government would bury him
　流浪漢死了 → 政府會埋葬他

◇ when a poor man died → the government would buy him a cheap coffin
　窮人死了 → 政府會幫他買便宜的棺材

如同 "can" 的過去式為 "could" 一般，"will" 的過去式為 "would"。

小試身手

3-1. 每次下雨，她就會借雨傘給我。

_____

3-2. 我小時候，我爸媽要求我先寫完功課才會讓我看電視。

_____

4. keep 維持；繼續（3 段）

The donor sent money to the government each year to keep the field looking nice.

(捐者)每年寄錢來，要求政府將這片草地維持得很好。

解析

直譯這句 "keep the field looking nice" 會得出：讓草地繼續顯得好看。（在中文原文裡，並沒有一個動詞接續「維持」；"look" 可粗略譯為「顯得」）這位捐者的目標是要維持一個良好的狀況。以下是 "keep" 在這用法中的另例：

◇ Our engineers keep our computer system running smoothly.
　　我們的工程師保持我們電腦系統的正常運作。

在這個用法中，"keep" 並不一定需要接續著以 ing 收尾的動詞。舉例來說，老闆可能會請她的員工要 "keep her informed"。換句話說，希望員工告知她所有該知道的資訊。通常當 "keep" 緊接著一個以 ing 收尾的動詞，用來表示 "continue"（繼續）：

◇ Keep running—you're almost to the finish line!
　　繼續跑啊，你快到終點線了！

在這法中 "keep" 比較正式且比 "continue" 更被廣為使用

小試身手

4-1. 那是我們最好的產品，它使我們能夠繼續營業。

_____

4-2. 你為什麼一直犯同樣的錯？

_____

(5) go on 進行（4 段）

He told me that his parents, when they were young, were attending a funeral at a mortuary when they discovered an extremely low-budget memorial service going on in the room next to them.

他說他的爸媽在年輕的時候，有一天去殯儀館參加一個葬禮，發現隔壁有一個非常簡陋的葬禮。

解析

這個片語中的 "on" 是「往前」的意思，如同電影鐵達尼號名曲 "My Heart Will Go On" 的歌名中 "on" 的用法一般。在英文裡我們說諸如喪禮等活動開始，"go on"（進行），而後結束。這個片語也同時能應用於形容對話與演說。

◈ I thought his speech would go on forever!
　我以為他的演講永遠講不完！

在口語中，這個片語可用於表示「發生了甚麼事」。

◈ What's going on with you guys?
　你們正在做什麼？

◈ Not much—we're just watching TV.
　沒什麼，我們只是在看電視。

另一個要注意的重點是：美國的殯儀館都是私有的建築，提供給人作為喪禮舉辦之用。在筆者家鄉，殯儀館看起來與教堂無異。雖然在美國其他地方有別的宗教盛行的殯儀館，或許以不同的外貌型態存在。但就我所知美國並沒有一個百分百與台灣殯儀館相同的地方。

另外，在抽象形容中，英文並沒有同中文裡「簡陋」一詞的形容詞。然而 "low-budget" 在故事中可扮演相同的角色。這個詞源自電影工業，導演們時常必須以極少的補助勉強度日

小試身手

5-1. 你有沒有看到市區正在進行的大型示威活動？

_____

5-2. 雨連續下了好幾天。

_____

5-3. 我朋友喜歡低成本的恐怖電影。

_____

---

(6) 以 "out of" 開頭的片語（6 段）

This seemed a little out of the ordinary, I thought.

我覺得這似乎有點不尋常。

解析

如果把 "the ordinary" 想成是可以用「尋常」形容的範圍，那就可以很容易理解是怎麼得出片語 "out of the ordinary"。在英文裡有許多片語是以 "out of" 開頭，像是 "out of sight, out of mind"（眼不見為淨）。以下舉一些實例：

out of the question	絕對不行
out of order	故障
out of one's mind	瘋了

小試身手

6-1. 哇，這冰淇淋好吃到不行！(不屬於這世界)

_____

6-2. 我不曉得它從哪來，它就這樣(從薄薄的空氣中)出現了。

_____

6-3. 不行，妳不可以陪妳男友去法國度暑假。這樣絕對不行。

_____

---

(7) turn into 使……變成(8 段)

It was she who had sent money to the cemetery to turn this plot of makeshift burial sites into a grass-covered graveyard.

是她寄錢給公墓，將這片亂葬之地變成了青草覆地的墓園。

解析

若你將 "turn" 這個片語想成「轉變」，就好記多了。從童話故事裡常可見到此片語的用法：

◇ The evil witch turned the prince into a frog.
邪惡的巫婆把王子變成青蛙。

小試身手

7-1. 原本以為會很簡單的方案已變成了物流上的 (logistical) 噩夢。

_____

7-2. 正面的態度能把挑戰化為機會。

_____

（8）whenever 每當；無論何時（10 段）

And now I have a strange tendency to think of my ancestors whenever I see a grassy field.

而且我有一個奇特的想法，每次看到青青的草原，我就會想到我的祖先。

解析

這個詞的兩個用法，和它的相關類詞 whatever, whoever, whomever, wherever 等等以下面實例做清楚的說明：

◈ Whenever I listen to classical music, I feel relaxed.
每當我聽古典音樂，就覺得很放鬆。

◈ It must be wonderful to be able to travel whenever you want.
隨時能出去旅行一定很棒。

◈ Whoever you are, you're not the person I'm looking for.
無論你是誰，你不是我要找的人。

◈ You can go to the dance with whoever you want.（因為是受詞，比較正式的英文可以用 whomever）
你想跟誰一起去舞會都可以。

> **小試身手**
>
> 8-1. 我買一盒任何一種你要的茶給你。
>
> _____
>
> 8-2. 無論你去哪裡,我們永遠在你背後。
>
> _____

(9) otherwise(不然)與假設語氣(10 段)

They are undoubtedly buried there—where would they be otherwise?

他們一定也是葬在草地之下,不然葬在哪裡呢?

解析

因這個句子的後半部是表示一個與前半部大不同的「想法」,後半部就必須為條件句。事實上,"otherwise" 這個字在此處的用法為「表示條件的」,雖然其條件程度可以不同的方式詮釋。舉例而言:

◇ We need to buy a flashlight—otherwise, what will we do if the power goes out?
我們需要買手電筒,不然停電了我們該怎麼辦?(對於未來的猜測)

◇ He was lucky he was wearing a helmet—the crash might have killed him otherwise.
他很幸運有戴安全帽,不然他可能在這場車禍中命喪黃泉(過去條件式,表示如果他沒有戴安全帽,也許會/也許不會命喪黃泉的可能性)

◇ He was lucky he was wearing a helmet—the crash would have killed him otherwise.
他很幸運有戴安全帽,不然他早就在這場車禍中命喪黃泉(過去假設,表示絕對)

從這些例子中我們可看出，如果「表示條件」的部分是「未來」，動詞通常不變；但若「表示條件／假設」的部分是「現在」或是「過去」，表示條件／假設的關鍵字諸如 "would" "could"或是 "might" 通常會出現在有 "otherwise" 的子句裡。

小試身手

9-1. 我希望那家餐廳還開著，不然我們可能得吃速食。

_____

9-2. 我想她應該在海邊。不然會在哪裡？

_____

小試身手解答

1-1. She calls herself a reporter, but she's really nothing more than a liar.

1-2. This is nothing less than a disaster.

2-1. He asked me if I'd like to go to a movie with him.

2-2. I wonder whether it will rain this weekend.

3-1. Every time it rained, she would lend me an umbrella.

3-2. When I was a kid, my parents made me finish my homework before they would let me watch TV.

4-1. That's our best product—it keeps us in business.

4-2. Why do you keep making the same mistake?

5-1. Did you see the big protest going on downtown?

5-2. The rain went on for days.

5-3. My friend loves low-budget horror films.

6-1. Wow, this ice cream is out of this world!

6-2. I don't know where it came from—it just appeared out of thin air.

6-3. No, you can't spend your summer vacation in France with your boyfriend. That's out of the question.

7-1. What I thought would be a simple project has turned into a logistical nightmare.

7-2. A positive attitude can turn a challenge into an opportunity.

8-1. I'll buy you a box of whatever kind of tea you want.

8-2. Wherever you go, we'll always be behind you.

9-1. I hope the restaurant is still open—otherwise we may have to eat fast food.

9-2. I think she's at the beach. Where would she be otherwise?

The Little Silver Box
小銀盒子

1-5　　　回想起來，這已經是五十年前的事了，當時我才從大學畢業，有人來找我，問我有沒有興趣去做當時教宗的貼身侍衛，教宗當然有貼身侍衛，而這些人是怎麼產生的？我從前一無所知，我從來沒有在報上看到這種找人的廣告，現在我知道了，教廷從不讓人申請，而是他們主動去找來的。我生長在一個天主教家庭，叔叔伯伯哥哥中都有人做了神父，我的一個妹妹做了修女，我的天主教信仰也算不錯的，大學成績很好，體育也很好，因此就有人來找我了。

　　　我一開始老大不願意，我認為這種工作高中畢業就可以去做了，我學的是生物，做這種事豈不奇怪？可是我知道教宗非常有智慧，而且也常常到外國去訪問，我為了滿足好奇心，就答應了。反正這是個四年的契約，我猜我做完四年以後就不會再做了。

　　　一開始，我當然有些緊張，教宗會忽然被一大批群眾包圍，雖然我受了好多的訓練，我根本弄不清楚誰是好人，誰是壞人。我知道，要想刺殺教宗，最簡單的辦法是穿上神父的衣服，如果打扮成主教就更

CD2-6

◇ bodyguard (n.) 保鑣；侍衛
◇ pope (n.) 教宗
◇ post (v.) 貼出；登(廣告)
◇ Holy See (n.) 教廷 (see＝主教的管轄區，亦稱為 diocese)

◇ prefer (v.) 寧願
◇ recruit (v.) 招募
◇ priesthood (n.) (泛稱)神職人員；神職職業
◇ faith (n.) 信仰

Looking back, it's been fifty years since these things happened. Back then, I had just graduated from college when a man came to see me, wanting to know if I would be interested in being a bodyguard for the pope. Obviously the pope has bodyguards, but where do they come from? Back then I had no idea—I had never seen an ad for the job posted in the newspaper. Now I know that the Holy See has never accepted applications, preferring instead to recruit candidates on its own. I grew up in a Catholic family: several of my uncles and older brothers had entered the priesthood, and one of my younger sisters was a nun. I was pretty strong in my Catholic faith, and I got good grades in college, especially in physical education. So they came to recruit me.

At first I was extremely reluctant. In my view, this was a job for a high school graduate, hardly a suitable career for a biology major like me. But I knew the pope had great wisdom, and he often visited foreign countries. To satisfy my curiosity, I said yes. In any case, it was a four-year contract—I figured I would do my four years and then move on.

Of course, in the beginning I was pretty nervous—all of a sudden the pope would be surrounded by a crowd, and though I had gone through extensive training, I hadn't the least idea to distinguish the good people from the bad people. I knew that the easiest way to

◈ reluctant (adj.) 不情願的
◈ suitable (adj.) 適當的
◈ major (n.) 主修(某學科)的人
◈ figure (v.) 想;忖度
◈ move on (v.) (告別過去而)向前
◈ surround (v.) 圍起來
◈ extensive (adj.) 大量的;大規模的
◈ distinguish (v.) 辨別

容易。教宗是個慈祥的人，他一直告訴我們不要緊張，如果有人刺殺了他，也絕不能用槍將對方殺死，只要使他不能再行兇就可以了。他們也都有禁令：絕對不可以先發制人。

有一天，教宗請我們所有侍衛吃晚飯，他說他對於這種保護實在感到很無奈，他又說他絕不會對刺殺他的人有任何怨恨，因為刺殺他的人，也是送他進天堂的人，他也絕對原諒任何這種人。教宗在飯桌上沒有任何訓話，反而和我們聞話家常，對我們每位侍衛的家人都很關心。我們事後都說教宗不是只關心我們靈魂的人，他對我們這些凡夫俗子的想法，顯然可以體會得到。舉例來說，他就很關心我們有沒有女朋友。

教宗每次出去，都要驚動義大利的警方，有時還要封鎖交通，警車開道是經常的事，對於這些擾民的事，教宗深感不安。他還有一個習慣，喜歡去訪問小教堂，可是每次訪問，都變成了大事，不僅大批警察出動，主教也一定會出來迎接。最後，教宗和大家取得一個協議，如果他去小教堂做彌撒，主教不必迎接，也不要任何一位主教陪同，

◇ assassinate (v.) 刺殺；暗殺
◇ robe (n.) 袍子
◇ kindly (adj.) 慈祥的(注意此字是形容詞等於 kind)
◇ strictly (adv.) 嚴格地
◇ forbid (v.) 禁止(注意不規則變化：forbid, forbade, forbidden)
◇ treat (v.) 請(客)
◇ cramp (v.) (過於)約束
◇ bear (v.) 懷有
◇ malice (n.) 怨恨
◇ forgive (v.) 原諒；寬恕
◇ lecture (n.) 訓話；演講
◇ engage (v.) 交流

assassinate the pope would be to dress in the robes of a priest, or
better yet, a bishop. The pope, a kindly man, frequently urged us not
to be nervous. He said that if someone did assassinate him, under no
circumstances were we to shoot to kill the assassin—all we had to
do was make sure he didn't kill anyone else. We were also strictly
forbidden to take the first shot.

One day the pope treated all of us bodyguards to dinner. He said he
felt cramped by all this protection and that he would bear no malice
toward any assassin, for that man would be the one who delivered
him to heaven, and he would surely forgive a man like that. At the
table, the pope had no lecture for us—he merely engaged us in casual
conversation, inquiring about our individual families. Afterward,
we noted he not only cared about the welfare of our souls, but could
even empathize with the thoughts of laymen like us. For example, he
wanted to know whether any of us had a girlfriend.

Whenever the pope went out, it was a quite a bother for the Italian
police. Sometimes we had to seal off roads, and being escorted by
patrol cars was commonplace. The pope had deep misgivings about
inconveniencing the people like this. Also, as a rule, he liked to visit
small chapels, but every time he did, it became a big to-do: the police

---

◈ welfare (n.) 福祉
◈ empathize (v.) 移情
◈ layman (n.)（天主/基督教用語）非神
　職人員
◈ bother (n.) 麻煩
◈ seal off (v.) 封鎖

◈ escort (v.) 護行
◈ patrol car (n.) 警車（patrol＝巡邏）
◈ misgiving (n.) 疑慮（通常用複數）
◈ as a rule (ph.) 一般來說
◈ to-do (n.) 忙亂的大事

義大利警察不必保護，也就是說，我們變成了唯一保護教宗的人。

6-10　　一開始，教宗出訪，仍有兩部車一起去，到後來，只有一部車了。我們的一位侍衛擔任司機，教宗和我們兩位侍衛共乘一部車，雖然義大利警方不再隨行，但是他們仍在重要的地方等我們的車子通過，我常常想，如果我們的車子沒有準時通過，很多人就會知道了。

　　雖然教宗本人對於安全保護越來越不在乎，我本人卻越來越擔心，因為當時巴勒斯坦問題非常嚴重，恐怖分子的活動也越來越猖獗，我常想，如果恐怖分子綁架教宗，一定會成為世界眾所矚目的大新聞。

　　有一天，我們又要到羅馬北部的一個小鄉村去，這種地方，過去的教宗是從來不會去的，可是教宗堅持要去，他好像非常喜歡到那些很荒涼的地方去，一來是因為他認為當地純樸的農民也有權利看到教

◇ in force (adv.) 大批
◇ compel (v.) 強迫
◇ compromise (n.) 妥協
◇ key (adj.) 關鍵的；重要的
◇ pass through (v.) 穿過
◇ reflect (v.) 省思
◇ fail (v.) 未；未能
◇ indifference (n.) 不在乎

would be out in force, and the local bishop would feel compelled to welcome the pope in person. Eventually, the pope and his associates reached a compromise: if he went to perform Mass at a small chapel, there was no need for a bishop to personally welcome him, or for a bishop to accompany him, or for the Italian police to provide security. In other words, we became the pope's only protection.

At first the pope's visits required two cars, but after a while only one was needed. One bodyguard would serve as driver, with the pope and two other bodyguards sitting together in the car. Although the Italian police no longer escorted us, they would still send people to key locations to wait for our car to pass through. I often reflected that if our car ever failed to pass through on time, a lot of people would know about it.

6-10

Despite the pope's increasing indifference toward his personal safety, I was getting worried. The problems in Palestine, I knew, were very serious, and terrorists were becoming ever more audacious. I often thought about the front-page news the terrorists would make if they kidnapped the pope.

One day we were set to visit a rural village north of Rome. His predecessors would never have gone to such a place, but the pope insisted. He appeared to particularly relish his visits to such desolate places, partly because he believed the unsophisticated farmers there

◈ audacious (v.) 膽大妄為的
◈ front-page news (n.) 頭條新聞
◈ kidnap (v.) 綁架
◈ predecessor (n.) 前任(不單指上一任)
◈ insist (v.) 堅持
◈ relish (v.) 打從心底的欣賞/享受
◈ desolate (adj.) 荒涼的
◈ unsophisticated (adj.) 純樸的

宗，二來他好像很喜歡看荒涼的鄉下景色，尤其是夕陽西下的景色。

當天，輪到我保護教宗，在路上，教宗除了不時小睡片刻以外，就和我們聊天，他對巴勒斯坦問題提出了很多非常特殊的想法，對我而言，這些見解使我茅塞頓開。

大約晚上五點半左右，天色已經昏暗，我們忽然看到前面有一個路障，司機只好被迫將車子停了下來，我一看，前後左右沒有一幢房子，也沒有一部車子，全是樹林，馬上就感到不妙，說時遲，那時快，兩個蒙面的人拿著衝鋒槍從附近的樹叢中走了出來，我們正準備拔槍，教宗卻叫我們不要動，他開了車門走了出去。 我們坐在車裡，看到教宗和這兩個恐怖分子講話，當然我們聽不見。不久，教宗回來了，他告訴我們，我們必須每一個人都睡一下，他說這兩個傢伙會給我們一種安眠藥吃，他向我們保證我們一定會醒過來的，我們當然相信他的話，但他的安危呢？教宗知道我們的憂慮，他一再安慰我們，一切都會有美好結局的，至於什麼是美好的結局，他沒有講，我們也不懂。

◇ landscape (n.) (陸地的)景色
◇ doze off (v.) 打盹
◇ dusk (n.) 黃昏
◇ set in (v.) 漸漸到來
◇ uneasiness (n.) 不安
◇ sweep (v.) 橫掃；席捲
◇ flash (n.) 閃光
◇ masked (adj.) 蒙面的

had a right to see the pope, and partly because he seemed to appreciate the beauty of a desolate rural landscape, especially as the sun set in the west.

That day it was my turn to protect the pope. On the way, when he wasn't dozing off, the pope chatted with us. He offered a remarkably unique view on the problems in Palestine that made me see the situation in a whole new light.

Around 5:30 in the evening, as dusk was setting in, we suddenly saw a roadblock ahead. The driver had no choice but to stop the car. I looked out but did not see a single house or car anywhere, only forest; immediately a feeling of uneasiness swept over me. Quick as a flash, two masked men with submachine guns emerged from the trees. We were about to draw our guns, but the pope ordered us not to move. He opened the car door and walked out. We sat inside the car, watching him speak with the two terrorists but of course unable to hear their conversation. Before long, the pope returned to tell us that we were all going to take a little nap. The two men would give us a kind of sedative, he said, promising that the sleep induced would be temporary. We believed him, of course, but what about the danger he was in? Knowing our concerns, he did his best to reassure us, emphasizing that there would be a happy ending to all of this. Exactly what he meant by a happy ending, he did not say, nor did we understand.

◈ emerge (v.) 出來
◈ draw (v.) 拔出 (武器)
◈ order (v.) 命令
◈ nap (n.) 小覺

◈ sedative (n.) 鎮靜劑；安眠藥
◈ induce (v.) 催生
◈ reassure (v.) 安慰
◈ emphasize (v.) 強調

11-15　　我們是晚上六點鐘吃下安眠藥的，一位蒙面的人拿了一罐藥，我們每人一顆，我記得我醒來的時候，已經是第二天的清晨六時，我睡去的地方，是在鄉下，醒來的地方卻是梵諦岡，一大堆的人在等我們清醒過來，義大利的警方也在場。

　　事後我才知道，我們的車子沒有按時經過一個義大利警方佈置的崗哨，他們立刻動員了一些警察去找。當時天色已經全暗，要找部汽車也不容易，大概在晚上八點鐘，我們的車在一條非常偏僻小路旁的樹林裡被找到了。我們三個活寶在車子裡呼呼大睡，教宗已經不見了。

　　梵諦岡在晚上八點半得知教宗失蹤的消息，教廷的發言人在羅馬晚上九點，向全世界宣佈教宗失蹤了，也請全世界的人為教宗祈禱。可是教廷的發言人也透露了一個消息，他說教宗曾經留下一份文件，這份文件中很清楚地說，萬一他被綁架，教廷絕對不要和綁架他的人有任何接觸，也絕對不能因為顧慮他的安全而和任何人妥協。教宗還有一個請求，萬一他因為綁架而去世，他要求全世界的各國政府絕對不要追查是誰幹的，他身為教宗，任務就是使世界更加友愛，更加和平，他只希望大家為他的靈魂祈禱，而不要關心他的安危，他絕對不

◈ pill (n.) 藥丸
◈ consciousness (n.) 清醒
◈ checkpoint (n.) 關卡
◈ mobilize (v.) 動員

◈ task (n.) 工作
◈ remote (adj.) 偏僻的
◈ snore (v.) 打鼾

It was 6:00 in the evening when we took the sedative. One of
the masked men brought over a bottle from which we each took
one pill. I remember that when I woke up, it was 6:00 the next
morning. I had fallen asleep in the countryside, but I awoke inside
the Vatican, surrounded by a crowd of people waiting for us to regain
consciousness, including the Italian police.

11-15

What had happened, as I later learned, was that when our car failed
to pass through an Italian police checkpoint on time, they immediately
mobilized a group of officers to look for us. By that time night had
fallen, and finding a car was no easy task. It was around eight in
the evening when our car was discovered in a forest beside a remote
country road. The three of us clowns were snoring away inside the
car, with the pope nowhere in sight.

The Vatican was notified of the pope's disappearance at 8:30 PM.
At 9 PM Roman time, a spokesman for the Holy See press secretary
announced to the world that the pope was missing and asked the
people of the world to pray for him. At the same time, however, the
press secretary divulged that the pope had left behind a document
stating quite explicitly that in the event of his abduction, the Holy
See was not to have any contact with his abductors or make any
compromises out of concern for his safety. In addition, the pope left
a request: if he died as a result of his abduction, the governments of

---

◇ away（adv.）（在 -ing 動詞之後）盡興
　地；不停地
◇ missing（adj.）失蹤的
◇ divulge（v.）透露

◇ explicitly（adv.）清楚地
◇ abduction（n.）綁架
◇ out of（ph.）出於

希望他的安危造成世界的不安。

在教廷宣佈教宗失蹤的消息以前，英國廣播公司搶先播報了這個新聞，他們推測綁架教宗團體是巴勒斯坦人，他們一定會要求以色列和美國在巴勒斯坦問題上讓步，否則就會殺害教宗。但教廷的宣佈卻使綁架的人無法得逞，果真沒有任何人向任何國家的政府提出要求，也沒有任何人承認是他們綁架教宗的。

我們三個人醒來以後，將我們所看到的據實以告，大概在清晨六點半，教廷接到了報告，有人找到了教宗。

16-20　　有一位義大利的農人，早上去牛廄裡去擠牛奶，發現教宗躺在草堆上，身上蓋了被，身旁有牛羊陪伴，好像安詳地睡著了，可是農人發現他已沒有呼吸，義大利的警方得到農人電話以後，立刻趕到了現場。不久一架直升機將教宗的遺體運回了梵諦岡。在梵諦岡，教宗的御醫和義大利最有權威的法醫都來了，大家的一致結論是教宗死於心

◇ investigate (v.) 調查；追究
◇ anxious (adj.) 著急的
◇ issue (v.) 發佈
◇ surmise (v.) 推測
◇ threaten (v.) 恐嚇；威脅
◇ concession (n.) 讓步

◇ doom (v.) 注定(悲慘的命運)
◇ scheme (n.) 計謀
◇ admit (v.) 承認
◇ relate (v.) 敘述
◇ hay (n.) (餵牲畜的)乾草
◇ wrap (v.) 包

the world must not investigate who was responsible. As the pope, his job was to make the world a friendlier, more peaceful place. He only wished that people would pray for his soul, not worry about his safety. The last thing he wanted was for the world to be anxious about his safety.

Even before the Holy See issued its announcement, the BBC reported the story of the pope's disappearance. They surmised that a group of Palestinians was responsible; no doubt they would threaten to kill the pope unless America and Israel made concessions on Palestine. But the Holy See's announcement had doomed their scheme to failure: no one demanded anything from any government, and no group admitted responsibility for the pope's kidnapping.

Once we regained consciousness, the three of us related what we had seen. Then, at around 6:30 AM, the Holy See received a report that the pope had been found.

As he went to the cowshed to milk his cows, an Italian farmer had discovered the pope lying on a pile of hay, his body wrapped in a blanket, as though slumbering serenely among the cows and sheep. But the farmer discovered he was not breathing. The moment they received the farmer's call, the Italian police rushed to the scene. Before long, a helicopter transported the pope's body back to the Vatican, where the pope's personal physician and Italy's preeminent

16-20

◇ blanket (n.) 毯子
◇ slumber (v.) 睡
◇ serenely (adv.) 安祥地

◇ transport (v.) 運送
◇ preeminent (adj.) 最卓越的；最知名的

臟病爆發，沒有任何他殺的跡象，教宗心臟不好，是眾所皆知的事，他死於心臟病，也是很正常的事。

教廷的主教們叫我們幾位侍衛進去，請我們檢查一下教宗身上有沒有任何東西不見了，教宗胸前的十字架仍然在，手指上的權戒也在，可是我發現有一件東西不見了，其他侍衛沒有發現這件事，我也沒有講，我當時有一個奇怪的想法，教宗是個思慮非常細膩的人，他的那個東西不見了，一定有原因的。

我們都參加了教宗的葬禮，葬禮中對他為何死亡，沒有一個人提及，主禮的樞機主教一再強調的是教宗熱愛和平，紀念他的最好方法就是致力於世人的和平相處。教宗就這樣離開了人世，誰都知道他是被綁架的，但是誰也不提究竟是什麼人做了這件事。

我呢？我離開了梵諦岡，回到大學去念研究所，拿到了博士學位，開始我的病理學教授的生涯。可是我一直懷念教宗，對我而言，他是個慈祥的老人，他關心所有的人，也就是他鼓勵我念博士學位的，我也常常去他的墳前去獻花。

◈ forensic (adj.) 法院的
◈ concur (v.) 同意
◈ heart attack (n.) 心臟病發作（attack＝攻擊）

◈ foul play (n.)（偵探用語）謀殺
◈ personal belongings (n.) 個人物品；隨身物品
◈ absence (n.) 不在；缺少

expert on forensic medicine concurred that he had died of a heart attack, with no sign of foul play. That the pope had a bad heart was common knowledge; it was a natural way for him to go.

The bishops at the Vatican called us in to check whether any of the pope's personal belongings were missing. The cross he wore over his chest was still there, as was the fisherman's ring on his finger. But I noticed the absence of something that the other guards overlooked. I didn't say anything, but I had a strange feeling that there must be a reason for its absence—the pope was not a man who would forget the detail like that.

We all attended the pope's funeral, but no one there mentioned the reason for his death. The archbishop who presided over the ceremony emphasized that given the pope's great love of peace, the best way to honor his memory was to help the people of the world learn to live together in harmony. And so it was that the pope departed from this world. Everyone knew he had been kidnapped, but no one mentioned who was responsible.

As for myself, I left the Vatican and returned to university for graduate school. I earned my Ph.D. and began a career as a professor of pathology. But I always cherished the memory of the pope. To me, he had been a kindly old man who cared for everyone. It was he who had encouraged me to get my Ph.D. I often brought flowers to his grave.

◈ overlook (v.) 看漏；忽略
◈ archbishop (n.) 樞機主教
◈ preside (v.) 主領；主禮
◈ ceremony (n.) 儀式；典禮

◈ honor (v.) 尊敬
◈ pathology (n.) 病理學
◈ cherish (v.) 珍惜

　　三十年過去了，有一天，我在看電視新聞，新聞中報導二位巴勒斯坦人得到了諾貝爾和平獎，其中一位是醫生，另一位是商人，他們得獎是因為他們一直在為巴勒斯坦的和平而努力。在記者招待會中那位醫生比較健談，他說三十年前，他們兩人都才從大學畢業，他們發現巴勒斯坦問題的癥結所在，在於巴勒斯坦人比以色列人窮太多了，在如此貧富不均的情況之下，巴勒斯坦人永遠有一股不平之氣，只要這股怨恨之情存在，巴勒斯坦就不會有和平。所以他們兩人都努力地改善巴勒斯坦人民的經濟狀況，也設法讓世人瞭解貧困常是紛爭的來由。在他們三十年來的努力之下，巴勒斯坦人的生活水準已經和以色列人相差不遠，這個地區的平靜也就跟著來了。

21-25　　我忽然想起了一些事，我覺得這位醫生的觀點我曾經聽到過，我知道他在黎巴嫩那一家醫院工作，我拿起筆來，寫了一封信給他，信中只有一句話，「小銀盒子是不是仍在你們那裡？」然後我註明我是當年教宗的侍衛，我的電話及通信地址。 果真，電話來了，醫生邀請我去看他。我們握手以後，他將小銀盒子交給了我。 教宗有心臟病，每天必須吃一種心臟病的藥，而我就負責將藥丸帶著，我有時會比教宗

◇ effort (n.) 努力
◇ achieve (v.) 成就；達成
◇ poverty (n.) 貧窮

◇ relative to (ph.) 相較於
◇ presence (n.) 存在
◇ inevitable (adj.) 難免的

Thirty years passed. Then one day while I was watching the news on TV, there was a story on two Palestinians who had won the Nobel Peace Prize. One of them was a doctor, the other was a businessman. They had been awarded the prize for their longstanding efforts toward achieving peace in Palestine. At the press conference, the doctor was the more talkative of the two. According to him, when the two of them graduated from college thirty years ago, they realized that the root of the Palestinian problem was the great poverty of the Palestinians relative to the Israelis. In the presence of such great economic inequality, it was inevitable that the Palestinians were always angry at what they perceived as injustice. As long as that resentment endured, there would be no peace in Palestine. So the two of them worked to improve the economic well-being of Palestinians and to make the world understand that conflict usually originates from poverty. Thanks to their three decades of work, the Palestinian standard of living is now almost as high as Israel's, and peace has come to the region as a result.

All of a sudden I realized I had heard the doctor's point of view 21-25 once before. Knowing the hospital in Lebanon where he worked, I picked up a pen and wrote him a letter consisting of just one sentence: "Do you still have the little silver box?" Then I explained that I had been one of the pope's bodyguards that day and wrote down my phone number and address. Just as I expected, the doctor called me on the phone and invited me to see him. We shook hands, and then he handed me a small silver box. The pope had suffered from a heart

◈ resentment (n.) 怨氣
◈ endure (v.) 持續
◈ conflict (n.) 衝突

◈ realize (v.) 發覺
◈ consist of (v.) 由……構成

早睡，體貼的教宗因此找到了一個小銀盒子，我負責將藥丸放進去，教宗會將小銀盒子隨身帶著。教宗死後，我當時就發現小銀盒子不翼而飛。

醫生告訴我，當他們綁架了教宗，教宗就立刻叫出了他們的名字，他說他們的組織早已被美國和以色列的情報人員滲透了。教宗和他的親信事先知道有兩位年輕人要來綁架他，他因此立刻通知以色列和美國政府，叫他們不僅當時不要作出反應，以後也不可以有任何反應，天主教會則是絕對只談愛，而不會使世界再增加絲毫仇恨的。教宗也告訴他們，他們的組織一旦發現無利可圖，就不會出面承認這件事的。問題是這兩個小子如何回去交代呢？

教宗提出了一個解套的方法，他只要一天不吃一顆心臟病的藥，就一定會死去，他拿出裝藥的小盒子，給了他們，叫他們丟掉，他今晚就會因為心臟病而去世，他們兩個人卻不是兇手，而且他又保證警方不會追查這件事的，因為這是他的願望。巴勒斯坦人一定以為教宗是自然死亡的。

◈ procure (v.) 取得（難找的東西）
◈ infiltrate (v.) 滲透
◈ intelligence (n.) 情報
◈ agent (n.) 特務
◈ associate (n.) 合作/交流的對象
◈ in advance (adv.) 事先
◈ contribute (v.) 貢獻
◈ spread (n.) 散佈；傳播

disease for which he had to take medication every day. I had been in charge of carrying his pills. Because I sometimes went to bed earlier than the pope, he was thoughtful enough to procure a little silver box. I would put the pill in the box, which the pope would carry with him. When he died, I discovered that the box had disappeared.

The doctor told me that during the kidnapping, the pope called him and his friend by name and said that their organization had been infiltrated by American and Israeli intelligence agents. The pope and his trusted associates had known in advance that these two young men were planning to abduct him, so he had immediately contacted the American and Israeli governments to request that they take no action, neither then nor later. The Catholic church was all about love; it would not contribute to the spread of hatred in the world. The pope also told the young men that their organization would not admit to the kidnapping once it discovered there was nothing to be gained from it. The problem was, how could they account for their failure when they got back to Palestine?

The pope offered them a way out. Knowing he would die if he did not take his heart pill that day, he took out the little silver box, gave it to them and told them to throw it away. That way, he would die of a heart attack that night, but the two of them would not be murderers, and he promised them that the police would not investigate further, for that was his wish. The Palestinians would surely think the pope had died of natural causes.

◈ account for（v.）解釋
◈ murderer（n.）殺人犯

◈ cause（n.）因素

　　可是，在臨死以前，教宗給他們講了一番大道理，他說巴勒斯坦的問題，在於巴勒斯坦人的經濟完全依賴以色列，以色列人有錢，巴勒斯坦人成為服侍以色列人的工人，因此他給他們一個命令，叫他們趕快離開，然後從此以後要致力巴勒斯坦人民生活的改善。

　　醫生和他的朋友少有開口的機會，他們一切都聽教宗的指示去做，他們本來就準備了一床厚厚的毯子，現在可以派上用場，教宗對於睡在稻草上感到很滿意，他們臨走以前，教宗給他們祝福，醫生忽然問他，「萬一我們不照你的意思做，你不是白死了嗎？」教宗的回答非常簡短，他說：「很少人不聽我的命令的。」

26-30　　醫生沒有丟掉小銀盒子，他相信教宗的話，警方不會追查這件事的，他也知道以色列和美國政府不會暗殺他，但是他們都留有遺囑，萬一他們被人暗殺，遺囑會公佈事情的始末。

　　醫生當然要問我一個問題，「你怎麼知道是我做的？」

　　我告訴他，當我拿到安眠藥膠囊的時候，膠囊外面有一個紙包，我拚老命記住藥名和廠牌，我事後發現這種藥只有醫生處方才會有，而

◇ dependence (n.) 依賴　　　　　◇ willingly (adv.) 心甘情願地
◇ devote (v.) 奉獻　　　　　　　◇ straw (n.) 稻草
◇ better (v.) 使……改善　　　　◇ bless (v.) 祝福

Before his death, however, the pope told them a great truth: the problems in Palestine, he said, were rooted in the Palestinians' total economic dependence on Israel. The Israelis had money, so the Palestinians became the workers who served them. In light of this, he ordered them to leave right away and devote themselves to bettering the lives of Palestinians.

The doctor and his friend hardly had a chance to speak. They followed the pope's instructions to the letter. Since they had brought a thick blanket with them, they put it to good use: the pope willingly lay down on a pile of straw to rest. As the two men were about to leave, the pope blessed them. Suddenly the doctor asked, "What if we don't do what you want us to? Will you not have died in vain?" The pope's answer was curt: "Few people ever disobey me."

The doctor never threw away the silver box. He believed what 26-30 the pope had said: the police would not investigate the incident, and the American and Israeli governments would not assassinate him. Nevertheless, he and his friend wrote wills so that in case they were assassinated, the truth would be known.

Of course, the doctor wanted to know, "How did you know it was me?"

I told him that the sleeping pill I took had been sealed in its original wrapping. Summoning all my mental strength, I memorized the name

◈ in vain (adv.) 徒然
◈ curt (adj.) 簡慢的;唐突的
◈ disobey (v.) 不聽話;違背

◈ will (n.) 遺囑
◈ summon (v.) 召集
◈ mental (adj.) 腦海的

且是中東地區的產品，當時那位蒙面的恐怖分子有一大罐，所以他一定是個中東地區的醫生。

最重要的是，他在記者會中的談話，正是教宗當天在汽車中和我們談的，我因此猜你們一定是又聽了教宗老人家的臨終訓話。

醫生將小銀盒子給了我，我接受了，他並沒有要求我保守祕密，因為他知道我會如此做的，他也好像不太在乎，因為教宗曾經謝謝他們，說是他們將他送入了天堂。

31-32　　我仍然保有這個小銀盒子，我會叮囑我的子孫，當我們這些當事人都去世以後，將小銀盒子送回給教廷，讓梵諦岡博物館保留它吧！這個小銀盒子離開了它的主人，卻帶來了中東的和平。

今早我又拿出了小銀盒子，我發現盒子底部有一句拉丁文的話，「惟有經過死亡，才能進入永生」。教宗顯然是一直能掌握自己命運的人。

◇ prescription (n.) 處方
◇ capsule (n.) 膠囊
◇ match (v.) 吻合；相配
◇ infer (v.) 推想

◇ act on (v.) 因……而採取行動
◇ secrecy (n.) 保密
◇ entrust (v.) 托給
◇ descendant (n.) 後代

and brand of the drug. Afterward I discovered that that particular drug was manufactured in the Middle East and could be obtained only by prescription. Since he had a whole bottle of the capsules, the masked man must have been a Middle Eastern doctor.

Most importantly, what he said at the press conference matched what the pope had told us in the car that night. So I inferred that he and his friend had acted on the pope's dying wish.

I accepted the gift of the silver box from the doctor. He didn't ask me to keep his secret, for he knew I would. At any rate, he didn't seem to care about secrecy, for the pope had thanked them for delivering him to heaven.

31-32

To this day I have kept the silver box. In the future I will entrust it to my descendants to return to the Holy See once all of the people involved in the affair have passed on. Let the Vatican preserve it in a museum! By leaving its rightful owner, that little silver box brought peace to the Middle East.

This morning when I took out the box, I discovered something written on the bottom in Latin: "Only through death," it read, "can one enter into eternal life." Clearly the pope had always been the master of his fate.

◇ involved (adj.) 有關連的
◇ preserve (v.) 保存
◇ rightful (adj.) 正當的
◇ eternal (adj.) 永恆的
◇ master (n.) 主宰

（1）用 "do" 或 "did" 加以強調（3段）

He said that if someone did assassinate him, under no circumstances were we to shoot to kill the assassin—all we had to do was make sure he didn't kill anyone else.

如果有人刺殺了他，也絕不能用槍將對方殺死，只要使他不能再行兇就可以了。

解析

為什麼原文句子要用 did assassinate 而不是只用 assassinated 呢？這是因為 did 可以表現出教宗口中的刺殺只是一個偶發事件，而不是必然會發生的事。它的意思比較像中文裡「萬一真的」。舉一個同樣的例子，想像你計畫在這個週末去遠足，氣象報告說當天的降雨機率為 20%，所以當天很有可能會是好天氣。但是萬一真的下雨的話（if it does rain），你就得預先做好下雨的準備。注意 "do" 或 "did" 後面要加原形動詞。

do 也可以用來指「是……沒錯」的意思，在小試身手裡你可以看到相關的例子。

小試身手

1-1. 甲：我以為你喜歡蘋果。

　　 乙：我是喜歡蘋果沒有錯，只是剛好不喜歡這一種。

　　 _____

　　 _____

1-2. 她說要是真的被裁員，她會回去學校。

　　 _____

（2） engage 交流（4段）

At the table, the pope had no lecture for us—he merely engaged us in casual conversation, inquiring about our individual families.

教宗在飯桌上沒有任何訓話，反而和我們閒話家常，對我們每位侍衛的家人都很關心。

解析

當你看到 engage 這個字時，你可能會先想到訂婚，但是這個字還有很多其他的意思，例如：

◈ He is engaged as Sir John's private secretary.
他是(被聘為)約翰爵士的私人秘書。

◈ During the Middle Ages, England and France engaged in several important wars.
英國和法國在中世紀發生(從事)了幾個重要的戰爭。

最近幾年也相當流行用 engage 這個字描述政治外交上的互動：例如美國一直以來都與中國有著建設性的交流(constructive engagement)政策。同樣地，如果你與某人從事(engage someone in)談話或對話的話，你就是在與他交流。

小試身手

2-1. 昨天我妹妹和他的未婚夫訂婚了。

_____

2-2. 歐巴馬總統已承諾和穆斯林世界進行對話。

_____

2-3. 兩位教授進行了熱烈(heated)的討論。

_____

（3）misgivings 不安的感覺（5段）

The pope had deep misgivings about inconveniencing the people like this.

對於這些擾民的事，教宗深感不安。

解析

雖然一開始看起來會覺得很奇怪，但是英文通常是用複數名詞來形容情感的。對於這些保護他而擾民的措施：警察必須要長時間工作，交通管制會耽擱當地駕駛的時間，主教們要在例行公事之間撥出時間來迎接他，教宗一定會有許多顧慮，因此他會感到種種不安，而不是只有單一不安。相同地，你或許也曾聽過有人這麼說：

◈ I have my doubts about his loyalty.
   我對他的忠誠有些懷疑。

小試身手

3-1. 我們的憂慮果然有理：新的老闆很霸道，正如我們所預料的。

_____

3-2. 牧師說上帝知道我們的喜悅與悲傷。

_____

3-3. 她對於為了家庭而放棄事業有些疑慮。

_____

(4) at first... after a while 一開始……到後來（6段）

At first the pope's visits required two cars, but after a while only one was needed.

一開始，教宗出訪，仍有兩部車一起去，到後來，只有一部車了。

解析

這是一個簡單又靈活的句型，相當值得大家記在腦海裡。它的用法不需要過多解釋，只要一個例句和幾則練習就已足夠。

◈ At first I was nervous in front of the class, but gradually I got used to being a teacher.
  一開始我在學生們的面前感到緊張，但我漸漸習慣了當教師。

注意 gradually（漸漸地）可以拿來替換 after a while。

小試身手

4-1. 隱形眼鏡一開始弄痛她的眼睛，可是到後來她幾乎忘了它們的存在。

_____

4-2. 一開始我們是陌生人，到了月底卻已變成朋友了。

_____

---

(5) 條件句過去式： if → would（6段）

I often reflected that if our car ever failed to pass through on time, a lot of people would know about it.

我常常想，如果我們的車子沒有準時通過，很多人就會知道了。

解析

如果我們把故事中的句子改成現在式的話，就會變成 If our car ever fails to

pass through on time, a lot of people will know about it.。但是既然故事主角用的時態是過去式，所以就得把 fails 改成 failed，而 will 要變成 would。現在看看這個句子：

◇ If no one has any questions, we can go home early.
　如果沒有人有償何問題的話，我們可以早點放學。

如果我們要將這個句子引用在過去式的話要怎麼做呢？

◇ The teacher said that if no one had any questions we could go home early.
　老師說如果沒有人有任何問題的話，我們可以早點放學。

小試身手

5-1. 醫生說如果我定期持續做運動的話，我可能可以活到 100 歲。

_____

5-2. 我告訴他就算他每天讀一本書，如果都不思考讀到的內容，也不會變得更聰明。

_____

---

(6) 「越來越」的不同譯法 (7段)

Despite the pope's increasing indifference toward his personal safety, I was getting worried. The problems in Palestine, I knew, were very serious, and terrorists were becoming ever more audacious.

雖然教宗本人對於安全保護越來越不在乎，我本人卻越來越擔心，因為當時巴勒斯坦問題非常嚴重，恐怖分子的活動也越來越猖獗。

解析

通常當我看到越來越_____時，我會譯成 "_____er and _____er"(用於單或雙音節形容詞)或是 "more and more _____"(用於雙音節以上形容詞)。

例如：

◈ （Example A）This road seems to get longer and longer.
這條路似乎變得越來越長。

◈ （Example B）As I watched the scary movie, I grew more and more afraid.
我看那部恐怖電影的時候，感到越來越害怕。

但是之後我覺得這個譯法單調乏味，而且也無法完全套用在有許多「越來越」的句子當中。還好，英文還有其他的方法可以表示相同的意義。首先得把形容詞變回原來的形式，然後在前面加 increasingly 這個字就行了。因此 Example A 就會變成：

◈ This road seems to get increasingly long.

Example B 變得更加流暢：

◈ As I watched the scary movie, I grew increasingly afraid.

把這個方法用在原文例句前段的話，就會變成：

◈ Although the pope was increasingly indifferent toward his personal safety...

但這個子句聽起來還是很累贅，所以我把「教宗本人對於安全保護越來越不在乎」這句改成名詞片語：“the pope's increasing indifference toward his personal safety.”，這樣一來這個子句就可以融入於更大的句子裡了。如果還是覺得很複雜的話，可以用相同的方法將上面的 Example A 和 B 改寫成名詞片語，看起來就會更簡單易懂了：

◈ the increasing length of this road

◈ increasing fear

你所要做的就是把形容詞改成名詞形式（long→length, afraid→fear），並且把 increasingly 字尾的-ly 去掉即可。

第二種翻譯越來越的方法是使用 "getting," "growing" 或 "becoming"。

◈ This road seems to be getting longer.

◈ The movie was growing scarier.

這個翻法可以合併 increasingly 使用：

◈ This road seems to be growing increasingly long.

◈ The movie became increasingly scary.

最後，如果你想要說越來越……以至於到相當高的程度時，你可以用 "ever" 或 "ever more"：

◈ This road seems to be growing ever longer.
這條路似乎長得永無止盡。

◈ As I watched the scary movie, I became ever more afraid.
我看那部恐部電影的時候，感到前所未有地害怕。

在寫作上能有多種選擇不是很好嗎？你有越多方法來表達一個意思，你就越有創造力。

小試身手

6-1. 世界經濟越來越複雜。

_____

6-2. 會議一直持續下去，而我越來越餓。

_____

6-3. 越來越熱的夏天使我們的電費高漲。

_____

（7）set to 安排；預定（8段）

One day we were set to visit a rural village north of Rome.

有一天，我們又要到羅馬北部的一個小鄉村去。

解析

假如你必須要在早上早起，你就會先設定(set)鬧鐘讓它在你要起床的時間響起。同樣地，這個用法也可以用在特定時間的活動排程上。例如老闆可能會對他的秘書這樣說：

◈ Boss: What's on the agenda for today?
今天的行程是什麼？

◈ Secretary: Well, you're set to meet with Mr. Kowalski in the morning and have lunch with the board of directors at noon.
嗯，早上你要和 Kowalski 先生見面，中午要和董事會吃飯。

小試身手

7. 甲：我們明天的行程，一切都準備好了嗎？

乙：嗯，我們預定早上六點出發。

_____

_____

（8）partly... partly 一部分是……而一部分是（8段）

He appeared to particularly relish his visits to such desolate places, partly because he believed the unsophisticated farmers there had a right to see the pope, and partly because he seemed to appreciate the beauty of a desolate rural landscape, especially as the sun set in the west.

他好像非常喜歡到那些很荒涼的地方去，一來是因為他認為當地純樸的農民也有權利看到教宗，二來他好像很喜歡看荒涼的鄉下景色，尤其是夕陽西下的景色。

解析

你為什麼要學英文？你的理由或許不只一個。除了工作上要用到英文外，你可能也愛看好萊塢電影。因此，當有人問你學英文的原因時，你可以回答：

◇ Well, partly because I need to read English at work, and partly because I like Hollywood movies.
　嗯，一方面是工作必須要讀英文，而另一方面是我喜歡好萊塢的電影。

要是其中某個理由比其他原因更重要呢？在這種情況下，你可以使用 mainly 來取代 partly：

◇ I'm learning English partly because I like Hollywood movies, but mainly because I need to read English at work.

此外，你也可以用 mostly。

> 小試身手
>
> 8-1. 我為什麼打羽毛球呢？一部分是因為對身體好，但主要是它很好玩。
>
> ＿＿＿＿＿＿＿＿＿＿＿＿＿＿＿＿＿＿
>
> 8-2. 我覺得大部分要歸咎於她，但我不否認我也該負一點責任。
>
> ＿＿＿＿＿＿＿＿＿＿＿＿＿＿＿＿＿＿

（9）when A wasn't ＿＿＿＿, he/she...

A 除了＿＿＿＿就……；只要不＿＿＿＿就……（9段）

On the way, when he wasn't dozing off, the pope chatted with us.
在路上，教宗除了不時小睡片刻以外，就和我們聊天。

解析

在搭車的期間，教宗不是和侍衛聊天就是小睡片刻。同樣地，世界上的人們也大多將時間花在從事兩者擇一的事情上。舉例來說，我叔叔喜歡釣魚，而且要是可以的話，他會把所有的時間都拿來釣魚。但不巧的是他也必須要工作，所以

◈ When he's not working, he's fishing.
　他只要不工作就去釣魚。

在大學時我有一個朋友非常喜歡玩電玩，愛玩到我要怎麼描述他？

◈ When he wasn't doing homework, he would play video games.
　他除了寫功課以外就玩電動。

小試身手

9-1. 她真是喜歡文字啊！不是在看小說就是在寫日記。

_____

9-2. (過去式)當他不忙於治理國家的時候，總統喜歡打高爾夫球。

_____

（10） see _____ in a new light 對_____另眼看待（9段）

He offered a remarkably unique view on the problems in Palestine that made me see the situation in a whole new light.

他對巴勒斯坦問題提出了很多非常特殊的想法，對我而言，這些見解使我茅塞頓開。

解析

我們看東西的角度取決於光線。一座森林在白天看起來靜謐又美麗，但到了晚上卻會讓人不寒而慄。而印象派畫家如莫內就藉由在一天中不同的時間

描繪相同景物，創造出極為不同的畫作。因此，to see something in a new light 就是指注意到以往未曾理解的事物面象。對於主角而言，教宗對於巴勒斯坦的看法改變了他原本的想法，將他原以為是複雜的問題轉變成簡單的原因。

就像大部分的英文句子一樣，這個用法也可以加以延伸。在《傲慢與偏見》一書中，伊莉莎白之所以不喜歡達西先生是因為他太傲慢，直到她知道一些事情讓她對達西先生投以不同以往或讚賞的眼光(a different or more favorable light)。又或者，倘若你不懂數學，你會請教對數學在行的朋友，請他幫你釐清(shed some light on)數學問題。

小試身手

10-1. 對我而言，這本傳記對皇后的描寫過於負面。

_____

10-2. 那個演講讓我對全球化完全另眼看待。

_____

---

(11) nor(也不)的用法(10段)

Exactly what he meant by a happy ending, he did not say, nor did we understand.

至於什麼是美好的結局，他沒有講，我們也不懂。

解析

像這樣的否定句不能用 also 來翻「我們也不懂」中的「也」。較好的選擇是只用 and 這個字來連接：

◈ He did not say, and we did not understand.

要處理第二個否定子句的最好用法是用 nor，但必須用倒裝的方法來寫，要把助動詞 did 移到 we 的前面，就像在寫以 not only 和 under no circumstances 為句首的句子一樣。以下兩個例子會讓意思清楚些：

◈ He doesn't like to talk, nor do I enjoy listening to him.
他不喜歡講話，我也不喜歡聽他講話。

◈ I've never been to Russia, nor have I ever been to Africa.
我沒去過俄羅斯，也沒去過非洲。

既然在語法上來說都是相同的，因此我們可以把接在 nor 後面的字當做是問句，用這個方法來記住它的文法規則就簡單多了。

小試身手

11-1. 至於生牛肉的口味怎麼樣，他沒告訴她，而她也不想知道。

_____

11-2. 雖然到亞利桑那州度假過一次，卻沒有參觀大峽谷（Grand Canyon），也沒有機會看響尾蛇隊（Diamondbacks）的球賽。

_____

---

(12) in the event of; in case 萬一（13段、26段）

...in the event of his abduction, the Holy See was not to have any contact with his abductors or make any compromises out of concern for his safety.
……萬一他被綁架，教廷絕對不要和綁架他的人有任何接觸，也絕對不能因為顧慮他的安全而和任何人妥協。

Nevertheless, he and his friend wrote wills so that in case they were assassinated, the truth would be known.
但是他們都留有遺囑，萬一他們被人暗殺，遺囑會公佈事情的始末。

解析

下次你搭飛機的時候，注意一下空服員的逃生解說，你很有可能會聽到這樣的説明：

◈ In the event of a water landing, your seat cushion can be used as a flotation device.
　萬一飛機在水面降落，你的坐墊可充當成浮具使用。

沒有人想要飛機在水面降落，但這種事發生的可能性還是會有的—不信的話可以問問 2009 年 1 月迫降在哈德遜河的人們。如你所見，in the event of 是用在極不可能發生的突發事件，如教宗被綁架或是飛機降落在水上。注意它後面接著的一定是名詞(即 of 的受詞)，但類似用法 in the event that 後面接著的則是子句，我們接下來會提及。

in case 也可以翻成「萬一」，但它後面一定是接完整子句。此外，in case 比較不正式，口語上較常使用，指的是有著相當高的可能性，而且可以出現在句子的後半部。舉例來説，假設一對夫婦要去參觀一個朋友的新家，這個地方他們從來都沒來過，這時太太可能會對先生説：

◈ We'd better take our cell phones in case we get lost.
　我們最好帶手機，萬一迷路〔就好解決〕。

下面這句聽起來比較奇怪，但文法上是正確的。

◈ In the event that we get lost, it would be good to have our cell phones.

小試身手

12-1. 萬一你好奇為什麼我昨天沒來上班，我生病了。

_____

12-2. 你最好把號碼記下來，免得忘記。

_____

12-3. 萬一發生火災，不要搭乘電梯。

_____

(13) doom to... 注定(悲慘的命運)(14段)

But the Holy See's announcement had doomed their scheme to failure.
但教廷的宣佈卻使綁架的人無法得逞。

解析

doom 當名詞時意味著死亡、毀滅、厄運或是世界末日，可以從有名的電影台詞 Prepare to meet your doom 得以證實。當動詞時，doom 有點像詛咒 curse 這個字，而且後面常接 to＋(不幸的命運)。例如：

◇ Those who do not learn from history are doomed to repeat it.
不汲取歷史教訓的人注定要重蹈覆轍。

◇ As soon as the general made that critical mistake, his army was doomed to defeat.
將軍一旦犯了那致命的錯誤，他的軍隊注定要敗北。

當然，誠如原文例句所示，doom 不侷限於指人一它也可以拿來指事物(主要是計畫、專案等)。

小試身手

13-1. 沒有良好的教育，你將注定終生貧窮。

_____

13-2. 由於老闆對那提案沒有興趣，它只有失敗的命運。

_____

(14) given 既然；以……為考量(18段)

The archbishop who presided over the ceremony emphasized that given the pope's great love of peace, the best way to honor his memory was to help the people of the world learn to live together in harmony.

主禮的樞機主教一再強調的是教宗熱愛和平，紀念他的最好方法就是致力於世人的和平相處。

解析

通常送禮都會有個送禮者(giver)與收禮者，但當 given 獨立存在的時候，它指的是事物存在的狀態，既不用知道它為何存在或是誰導致它變成這樣。邏輯上，given 後面接著的是為之後結論預設的前提。在這個故事裡，它的邏輯是這樣的：

◇ The pope loved peace; therefore, the best way to honor his memory is to work for peace.

為什麼教宗熱愛和平？這並不是我們探討的重點—重點應該是我們要怎麼做才能合乎教宗熱愛和平的特質。

因此 the pope love peace 就可以改寫成陳述事實的名詞片語，然後前面加個 given 當作結論的根據。

另外舉個例子，假設你是一個秘書，你的老闆擁有一間大公司而且相當富有，他想要買一台新的私人噴射機，但是你覺得應該要提醒他現在市道不好，而且這樣的舉動會帶給員工不好的觀感，因為員工會覺得這是奢侈的花費。這時你要怎麼對你的老闆說？

◇ Given the current state of the economy, I don't think buying a new private jet would be a wise idea.
　以現在的經濟狀況為考量，我認為買一台新的私人噴射機並非明智之舉。

當然，如果你的老闆不喜歡人家冒犯他的話，你就不應該多說什麼。當他買了新噴射機後，公司員工向你抱怨時，你可以這麼說：

◈ Given the boss's touchiness about criticism, I decided it would be a bad idea to protest.
既然老闆禁不起批評，我認為揭竿抗議是個壞主意。

小試身手

14-1. 既然她有不誠實的名聲，我建議我們改選不同的合夥人。

＿＿＿＿＿＿＿＿＿＿＿＿＿＿＿＿＿＿＿＿＿＿＿＿

14-2. 政府浪費這麼多錢，納稅人為什麼沒有生氣？

＿＿＿＿＿＿＿＿＿＿＿＿＿＿＿＿＿＿＿＿＿＿＿＿

---

(15) It was he who 就是他(做了某件事) (19段)

It was he who had encouraged me to get my Ph.D.
也就是他鼓勵我念博士學位的。

解析

當你想要用中文強調句子的主詞時，你可以用「是」或「就是」：

就是她教我成功的意義。

英文也多少有點類似，但有一件事要注意的是英文不用受格代名詞(me, her, him 等)來當作主詞：

◈ It was she who taught me the meaning of success.

然而，當主詞後面沒有接任何東西的時候，大部分的人卻會用受格代名詞：

◈ A: Who messed up this room?
誰把這間房間弄亂了？

◈ B: It wasn't me!
不是我！

小試身手

15-1. 是我警告他他的老闆不老實。

_____

15-2. 問：這場架是誰先動手的？

　　　答：是他們。

_____

_____

---

(16) 二者的比較(20段)

At the press conference, the doctor was <u>the more talkative of the two.</u>
在記者招待會中那位醫生比較健談。

解析

首先，我要先提醒大家，如果只有兩件事物相比的時候，不能用最高級形容詞，像在這裡如果用 most talkative 的話就錯了。只有兩件事物相比的好處在於能藉由使用「the＋比較級」的形式指涉兩者其中之一並把它當作名詞。上面原文例句標示的部分翻得白話一點的話，就可以翻成：

二者當中較為健談者

句中的 the 就像在中文裡加了「者」。在正式英文中，前者 the former 和後者 the latter 就是這個原理的好例子：

◇ Tyler and Cory were brothers: the former was a businessman and the latter was a construction worker.
Tyler 和 Cory 是兄弟：前者是生意人，後者是建築工人。

16-1. 姐姐是金髮的，而妹妹有咖啡色的頭髮。

_____

16-2. Jesse 是四人當中最兇狠的。

_____

(17) relative to 相較於（20段）

They realized that the root of the Palestinian problem was the great poverty of the Palestinians relative to the Israelis.

他們發現巴勒斯坦問題的癥結所在，在於巴勒斯坦人比以色列人窮太多了。

解析

貧窮是相對的概念，如果全世界的人一天都只賺一美金的話，沒有人會被認為是貧窮，因為沒有更高的生活水準可供比較。但是根據教宗的言論，巴勒斯坦人之所以覺得貧窮是因為鄰近的以色列人太富有了。所有的比較一定都是相對於（relative to）某些標準，否則就毫無意義。問題是要相較於什麼？回答這個問題時，要知道 compare with 經常可以拿來代替 relative to。

17-1. 跟平常因節儉的預算而買的便當相比，那頓晚餐很好吃。

_____

17-2. 對我們來說地球好像極大，但相較於太空的廣闊（vastness），它微不足道。

_____

（18）**thanks to** 虧得；由於（20段）

Thanks to their three decades of work, the Palestinian standard of living is now almost as high as Israel's, and peace has come to the region as a result.

在他們三十年來的努力之下，巴勒斯坦人的生活水準已經和以色列人相差不遠，這個地區的平靜也就跟著來了。

解析

thanks to 本質上等於 because of，但是意思上則另外帶有讚許或感激之意。藉由使用這個片語，主角暗示著他讚美醫生行善。另外還有一個例子，想像你發生了車禍，一個陌生人經過救了你，你們的對話可能是：

◈ Stranger: Are you all right?
你還好嗎？

◈ You: Yes, I'm fine, thanks to you.
嗯，我還好，多虧你幫忙。

注意 thank to 也可以用在諷刺揶揄上：

◈ Thanks to this snowstorm, we're going to miss our flight.
由於這個暴風雪，我們就要錯過我們的飛機了。

小試身手

18-1. 昨天由於總統的經濟振興方案，股價上漲了。

_____

18-2. 因為愛迪生，現在我們晚上不用點蠟燭了。

_____

（19） all about 非常重視；一切都和……有關(22段)

The Catholic church was all about love; it would not contribute to the spread of hatred in the world.

天主教會則是絕對只談愛，而不會使世界再增加絲毫仇恨的。

解析

這是一個簡短、口語的句型，用來表示天主教會所做的每件事都是基於愛。在現代英文裡，使用 all about 已經變成了一種流行，而且常出現在歌名中，像吹牛老爹的 "It's All About the Benjamins"，這裡的 Benjamin 指的就是 $100 鈔票上面的 Benjamin Franklin。另外一個例子常出自於運動主播口中：

◈ At this stage in the game it's all about guts and determination.
　比賽到了這地步，一切都靠魄力和毅力。

然而，這種用法更常用於單指「一個人想知道的所有事情」，就像 Tell me all about it! 的用法一樣。

小試身手

19-1. 我們公司非常重視客服。

_____

19-2. 我想知道你這次約會的點點滴滴！

_____

小試身手解答

1-1. A: I thought you liked apples.

　　 B: I do like apples, just not this particular kind.

1-2. She said that if she did get laid off, she would go back to school.

2-1. Yesterday my sister got engaged to her fiancé.

2-2. President Obama has promised to engage in dialogue with the Muslim world.

2-3. The two professors engaged in a heated discussion.

3-1. Our fears proved to be justified: the new boss was a tyrant, just as we had expected.

3-2. The pastor said that God knows our joys and sorrows.

3-3. She felt some misgivings about giving up her career for her family.

4-1. The contact lenses hurt her eyes at first, but after a while she hardly noticed them.

4-2. At first we were strangers, but by the end of the month we had become friends.

5-1. The doctor said that if I continued to exercise regularly, I might live to be 100.

5-2. I told him that even if he read a book every day, if he didn't think about what he read, he wouldn't get any smarter.

6-1. The world economy is growing ever more complex.

6-2. As the meeting went on and on, I was getting hungry.

As the meeting went on and on, I was becoming increasingly hungry.

6-3. The increasing summer heat caused our electric bill to go up.

7. A: Is everything ready for our trip tomorrow?

B: Yep, we're set to depart at 6 AM.

8-1. Why do I play badminton? Partly because it's good for me, but mainly because it's fun.

8-2. I think she is mostly to blame, but I won't deny that I'm partly responsible too.

9-1. She sure loves words! When she isn't reading a novel, she's writing in her diary.

9-2. When he wasn't busy running the country, the president liked to play golf.

10-1. In my view, this biography portrays the queen in an overly negative light.

10-2. The lecture made me see globalization in a totally new light.

11-1. As for what raw beef tasted like, he did not tell her, nor did she want to know.

11-2. Although I once went on vacation to Arizona, I did not visit the Grand Canyon, nor did I have a chance to see a Diamondbacks game.

12-1. In case you were wondering why I wasn't at work yesterday, I was sick.

12-2. You'd better write down the number in case you forget.

12-3. In the event of a fire, do not take the elevator.

13-1. Without a good education, you'll be doomed to a life of poverty.

13-2. The boss's lack of interest in the proposal doomed it to failure.

14-1. Given her reputation for dishonesty, I suggest we choose a different partner.

14-2. Given the amount of money the government wastes, why aren't taxpayers more angry?

15-1. It was I who warned him that his boss was dishonest.

15-2. Q: Who started the fight?

A: It was them.

16-1. The elder sister is blond, while the younger has brown hair.

16-2. Jesse is the meanest of the four.

17-1. The dinner was delicious relative to the boxed meals I typically buy on my tight budget.

17-2. To us the earth seems enormous, but compared with the vastness of space, it is nothing.

18-1. Stock prices were up yesterday thanks to the president's economic stimulus package.

18-2. Thanks to Thomas Edison, we no longer have to light candles at night.

19-1. Our business is all about customer service.

19-2. I want to know all about your date!

Afterword
跋

Nick Hawkins

CD2-7

All good things must come to an end: our *Read R.C.T. Lee, Learn English* series has finally drawn to a close. Besides enjoying Professor Lee's wonderful stories, I hope you have improved your English. This is the biggest project I have ever worked on; among all the changes of the past three years of my life, it has always been with me. Because of all the hard work I've put into these seven books, they are very meaningful to me. And I'm convinced that as long as you really study each book, doing all the practice translations, memorizing all the sentence patterns, remembering all the vocabulary, and (perhaps most importantly) savoring all the pleasures of learning, then there is no reason to doubt that you will benefit. As the proverb says, as you sow, so shall you reap.

Learning a foreign language is a lot of work, but if you do it right you'll be rewarded. As long as you take the right approach and stick with it, not only will you give yourself opportunities you never dreamed of, you'll have a great time as well. However, if you're too casual or too lazy, you'll only end up squandering time and money. Let me illustrate: I took two years of Spanish in junior high and another year in high school, but I never spoke the language outside of class. I had no Spanish-speaking friends and no desire to visit any part of the Spanish-speaking world—all I was trying to do was fulfill a requirement for applying for college. As a result, all I learned was vocabulary and grammar, not a language. What a waste! All over America, the Hispanic population is growing enormously, mainly

郝凱揚

(本文由郝凱揚自行由英文譯成中文，以供讀者參考)

　　天下沒有不散的筵席；我們的《讀李家同學英文》系列終於圓滿結束了。除了欣賞李教授的精彩故事以外，我希望對你的英文有所改善。這是我一生中參與過最大的工程，三年來的萬變之中，它一直都陪伴著我。由於我投入了許多心血，這七本書對我的意義十分重大。而我相信，只要你好好地研讀每一本，將每題小試身手都寫好，該背的句型都背熟，該記的單字都記牢，而(或許最重要地)該欣賞的妙趣都欣賞，那麼不用怕沒有益處。所謂一分耕耘，一分收穫也。

　　學好一個外語需要相當地努力，但如果做的對你就會有收穫。只要你採取正確的方法並持之以恆，你不但會帶給自己做夢也沒想過的機會，還會學得很愉快。然而，假如你太隨便或太懶惰，到最後你只會揮霍時間和金錢。容我舉自己的例子闡明：我國中修過兩年的西班牙語，高中又修了一年，但除了課堂上以外我從來不說西語。我一個講西語的朋友都沒有，也沒有渴望到西語世界任何一個地方去，我只要完成申請大學的要求，這樣而已。結果，我學到的只是單字和文法而非一個語言。多浪費啊！現在美國講西語的人口到處暴增，主要是由於墨西哥來的移民(合法和非法都有)。在我的故鄉猶他州，有墨西哥的建設工人，墨西哥的清潔人員，墨西哥的廚師，墨西哥的大學生，甚至墨西哥的電視節目。他們有一整個次文化，對此文化，一般的白

due to immigration from Mexico (both legal and illegal). In Utah, my home state, there are Mexican construction workers, Mexican janitors, Mexican cooks, Mexican college students, even Mexican TV shows. They have a whole subculture that most of the white population cannot even begin to understand. If I had learned Spanish when I had the chance, I could have been a part of that culture. But I did not, and now I am nothing more than a curious outsider.

On the other hand, it took me just six months to become fairly fluent in Chinese. In my church's Missionary Training Center in Provo, Utah, I had eight or nine hours of class per day, five days a week, for eleven weeks. Then I was sent to downtown Taipei and told to spread the gospel to Taiwanese people for ten hours a day. The only American I got to talk to was my companion (missionaries serve in pairs), who could help me with Mandarin because he had already been in Taiwan for over a year. Probably the greatest motivation I had to learn was the frustration I felt at not being able to communicate with the people around me. I remember one night when a woman asked a question to my companion after they had been talking for a minute or two. Overjoyed that I actually understood her question, I answered her in Chinese. She took one look at me and said: "Your Chinese isn't as good as his." Then she went on talking with my companion, as if I didn't exist. Maybe she was telling the truth, or maybe she was just being rude—at any rate, I knew I never wanted to hear those words again. And I never did.

Of course, unless you want to knock on doors in America for two years as a missionary (or perhaps a salesperson), you'll probably

人陌生到不行。假如我當時把握機會學好了西班牙語，我就能融入那個文化。但是我沒有，因此我現在只不過是個好奇的旁觀者。

　　相反地，學會講相當順暢的中文僅僅花了我六個月的時間。在我教會位於猶他州Provo的傳教士訓練中心，我一天有八、九個小時的課，一週五天，總共十一週。然後我被派去台北的市區，奉命對台灣人傳福音，每天傳十個小時。陪我講話的美國人只有一個，就是我同伴(傳教士兩人一組)，因為他已在台灣待了一年多，他能輔導我學中文。我最強的學習動力大概是無法和周遭的人溝通所帶來的挫折感。記得有一天晚上我同伴和一位太太聊了一兩分鐘，然後那位太太問他一個問題。我竟然因為聽懂了他的問題而大喜過望，於是用中文回答她。她看了我一眼就說，「你的中文比較不好。」然後她繼續和我同伴說話，彷彿我不存在。也許她說得對，也許她不過是對我無禮，反正我知道我再也不想聽到那些話。而我再也沒有聽過這類評語。

　　當然，除非你想去美國當傳教士(或許推銷員也行)敲兩年的門，你大部分的英文恐怕要在台灣學。這樣不容易，但是並非不可能：我

have to learn most of your English here in Taiwan. This is not easy, but it is possible—I've met quite a few good English speakers who have never left Taiwan. If you want to learn English, you need to be motivated, work hard and stick with it: don't memorize vocabulary for a month and then spend the next week forgetting it. Here are some things you might want to try:

Taking a class. It's much easier to learn a language with a teacher than by yourself, especially when you want to practice conversation. Not all classes are helpful, though—make sure you choose a teacher who gives you a chance to talk. I can't emphasize this enough. It's no good to sit for an hour listening to your teacher speak English— you need to speak it yourself. The best classes are small—ideally no more than five students—and focused on improving your ability to speak English, not helping you get a good score on a test. (If English education in Taiwan was less about tests and more about actual ability, the Taiwanese would speak much better English.) Don't forget that there is more to conversation than fluency: classes make an excellent setting to correct grammatical bad habits.

Hiring a tutor. This is expensive, but tutors can help you in ways that classes can't. For example, they can correct mistakes you make in your writing, tailor lessons to your areas of interest (business, TV, detective stories, etc.), and help you apply for graduate school. If you can't afford to hire a good tutor, you may want to consider doing a language exchange, although this will only work well if you and your partner both take it seriously.

遇過不少英文好卻沒有出過國的台灣人。若你想學好英文，你要有動力，要下功夫，而且要持之以恆：不要花一個月背單字然後花一個禮拜忘記。以下謹列出一些你可以嘗試的辦法：

上課。跟著老師學比無師自通要來得容易，尤其是在練習會話方面。然而，不是全部的課程都有益處：一定要選一個給你機會講話的老師。我必須再次強調這點。坐著聽老師講一個小時的英文沒有用──你需要自己講。最好的課程採用小班制(理想上以五人為限)，重點放在改善你的英文會話能力而不是教你考試考高分。(要是台灣的英文教育講究實力而不是考試，台灣人的英文一定會更好。)別忘記，會話不只靠流利：上課可提供非常適合改掉文法惡習的環境。

請家教。這樣有點貴，但是家教能提供你在課堂上得不到的幫助。例如，他們可以改正你寫作的錯誤，因應你的興趣(商業，電視，偵探小說等)而施教，以及協助你申請研究所。假如你請不起一個好家教，或許可以考慮語言交換，然而這種安排需要雙方都很認真才能成功。

Attending a short-term language program in an English-speaking country. If you are a student, you can do this during your summer vacation; if you work full-time, it wouldn't kill you to take a few weeks off. Intensive language programs eliminate distractions, allowing you to focus all your attention on English, while the foreign environment accelerates the speed at which you absorb what you learn.

Reading a book in English. I still remember the thrill I felt when I finished my first real book in Chinese, a collection of six short stories by Lu Xun, including "The True Story of Ah-Q," that I borrowed from the Stanford library. Not long after, I took up Jin Yong's martial arts novels, whose titles sound ridiculous in English: The Condor-Shooting Heroes, The Chivalrous Companions of the Divine Condor, The Deer and the Cauldron (which actually has a published English translation—I've seen it in bookstores). At first I had to look up so many words in the dictionary that I filled an entire notebook with vocabulary, but in the end all that tedious effort paid off. Now I can read 100 pages of Jin Yong in a single day without the aid of a dictionary—context is usually sufficient for me to figure out the meaning of the few expressions I do not know. From these books I've picked up everything from historical knowledge to swear words.

There is no reason why you can't do the same thing with English. Reading is supposed to be fun! Instead of trying to memorize a boring list of hundreds of vocabulary words in alphabetical order, find a good story and learn to appreciate it without the filter of translation. (Just like Jin Yong's work doesn't translate well into English.) If you like fantasy, try Harry Potter; if mystery is your thing, check out Agatha

參加英語系國家的短期語言研習班。如果你是學生，暑假就可以去；如果有全職的工作，請幾個禮拜的假也死不了人。上密集語言研習班可排除雜事，使你能夠全心專注於英文，而國外的環境會加快你吸收知識的速度。

閱讀一本英文的書。我到現在還記得看完第一本真正的中文書的那股興奮，那書我從史丹佛的圖書館借出來的，裡面收集了魯迅的六篇故事，包括《阿Q正傳》。不久之後，我拿起了金庸的武俠小說，他的書名譯成了英文聽起來很好笑：《射鵰英雄傳》、《神鵰俠侶》、《鹿鼎記》(其實這本有出英文翻譯，我在書店裡看過)。一開始我得查字典查到整個筆記本都寫滿了生詞，但是到後來那許多枯燥的努力帶來了很大的收穫。現在我不靠字典就能一天讀一百頁的金庸：寥寥幾個不懂的字眼，通常可以從上下文猜出意思來。從這些書中我學到了各種東西，從歷史知識到髒話。

你用同樣的方式學英文沒什麼不可。閱讀應該是一種樂趣才對！與其要背幾百個一成串從A到Z的無聊單字，不如找一篇精彩的故事，學會不透過翻譯的來欣賞它。(正如金庸的作品不太能譯成英文，我很難相信《魔戒》變成中文還能保留原味。)如果你喜歡幻想，嘗嘗《哈利波特》；對推理感興趣，看看阿嘉莎·克莉絲蒂(李教授也推薦過)或是創造福爾摩斯的柯南道爾爵士；迷戀吸血鬼，就拿起《暮光之城》

Christie (also recommended by Professor Lee) or Sir Arthur Conan Doyle, creator of Sherlock Holmes; if you're into vampires, read the Twilight series. No matter what you're interested in, I guarantee that someone has written something about it in English.

The next time you have a free afternoon, find a good bookstore and browse through the English book section. Find a book that catches your eye, buy it, take it home, sit down on the couch with your best dictionary and a notebook open beside you, and prepare to enter a whole new world.

I hope that through these books Professor Lee and I have managed to infect you with our passion for English. With us, you have traveled from the wilds of Africa through the hallowed halls of the Vatican to the mountains of familiar Taiwan. If his stories and my translations have sparked your imagination, let that motivate you to continue your studies. The better your English gets, the more fascinating your world will become.

系列。無論你的興趣為何，我保證一定有人用英文寫過相關的作品。

　　下次遇到閒閒無代誌的下午，去找家好書店，瀏覽那邊的英文書。找一本讓你眼神一亮的書，買它，把它帶回家，坐在沙發上，把你最好的字典和一本筆記本攤開在旁，然後準備進入一個嶄新的世界。

　　希冀藉著這幾本書，我和李教授成功地將我們對英文的熱情感染給你了。以我們為導遊，你已從非洲的荒野旅行到梵蒂岡的聖堂，又回到熟悉的台灣山區。假如他的故事和我的翻譯有激發你的想像力，讓這樣變成你繼續學習的動力。隨著你的英文越來越好，你的世界將變得越來越精采。

Linking English
讀李家同學英文7：小男孩的爸爸

2009年6月初版　　　　　　　　　　　　　　　　定價：新臺幣320元
2021年3月初版第三刷
有著作權・翻印必究
Printed in Taiwan.

著　　者	李　家　同	
譯　　者	Nick Hawkins	
解　　析	Nick Hawkins	
叢書主編	陳　若　慈	
校　　對	劉　力　銘	
	曾　婷　姬	
封面設計	翁　國　鈞	
內文排版	陳　如　琪	

出　版　者	聯經出版事業股份有限公司	副總編輯	陳　逸　華
地　　　址	新北市汐止區大同路一段369號1樓	總　編　輯	涂　豐　恩
叢書主編電話	(02)86925588轉5305	總　經　理	陳　芝　宇
台北聯經書房	台北市新生南路三段94號	社　　長	羅　國　俊
電　　　話	(02)23620308	發　行　人	林　載　爵
台中分公司	台中市北區崇德路一段198號		
暨門市電話	(04)22312023		
郵政劃撥帳戶第0100559-3號			
郵撥電話	(02)23620308		
印　刷　者	文聯彩色製版印刷有限公司		
總　經　銷	聯合發行股份有限公司		
發　行　所	新北市新店區寶橋路235巷6弄6號2F		
電　　　話	(02)29178022		

行政院新聞局出版事業登記證局版臺業字第0130號

國家圖書館出版品預行編目資料

讀李家同學英文7：小男孩的爸爸 /
李家同著 . Nick Hawkins譯/解析
初版 . 新北市 . 聯經 . 2009.06
208面 . 14.8×21公分 . (Linking English)
ISBN　978-957-08-3433-8（平裝）
[2021年3月初版第三刷]

1.英語　2.讀本

805.18　　　　　　　　　　　98009579